TANDEM

Ice Bomb Zero

A frozen setting . . .

Somewhere in the coldest and most desolate real estate on earth the Chinese have hidden a deadly missile base. A serious threat to the balance of power, it has to be found and destroyed – despite screaming blizzards, prowling bears, a fool-proof Chinese defense system, and a very touchy Soviet-American partnership.

A lukewarm alliance . . .

When AXE tells Nick Carter he will be working with a female operative from the Other Side, he is steeled for the worst. Both agents are pros and soon develop a cautious respect for each other. Besides, she is beautiful, Nick is Nick, and where they are going the nights are long and cold.

Boiling suspense . . .

Between the lethal environment, a treacherous ally, and the ferocious Chinese crack troops, Nick has an eerie feeling that this is the mission he won't escape alive.

Ice Bomb Zero

Nick Carter

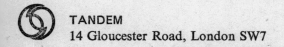

TANDEM
14 Gloucester Road, London SW7

Originally published in the United States by Universal
Publishing and Distributing Corporation, 1971

Published in Great Britain by Universal-Tandem Publishing
Co. Ltd, 1972
Reprinted December 1972

Dedicated to
The Men of the Secret Services
of the
United States of America

Made and printed in Great Britain by
Hunt Barnard Printing Ltd., Aylesbury, Bucks.

ONE

The world is shrinking for me, it's running out of intimate little hideaways. Each time I get a few days or a couple of weeks to myself where I can enjoy life, there is nowhere to go.

This time I wanted a climate as close to California as possible—sunshine, soft breezes—but without the smog and without the people. I found it.

I was staying at the Calvi Palace, in Calvi, which is on the island of Corsica in the Mediterranean. The young lady's name was Sonja. Sonja Treshenko. Somehow we had found a court to play tennis on.

Blue mountains rose steeply behind us, high over Calvi's beach-rimmed peninsula. Calvi itself is a walled, medieval town. It is dominated by a Genoese citadel. As the story goes, a bunch of Russians landed there sometime in the '20s determined to live the "good life." Their descendants still dominate the population, so a name like Sonja Treshenko was not out of place. On summer nights, when Calvi pulsates with people, you can see the Russians dancing in the streets to the accompaniment of accordion and guitar. In Russian-run clubs like the Chez Tao, or under the Old Town ramparts, men and women drink, dine and dance until dawn. From May until September, Calvi is one of the liveliest small resorts in Europe. A lot of this is helped by the presence of a foreign legion post nearby.

So far Corsica's savage scenery and primitive pleasures have preserved it from the tourist stampede which has transformed so many other Mediterranean beauty spots. But, gradually, there have emerged car-carrying ferries and new, ultra-modern hotels, adding expense and luring more tourists. Corsica, I'm afraid, is going down the same trail so many other lovely Edens have gone—a trail lined with outstretched hands trying to seize the almighty dollar.

But not quite yet. There is still plenty of primitive charm left, particularly when the tourist season is over. It was November now, and there I was, playing one more game of tennis with a delicious young woman.

Sonja had already served. This was our third game and it was almost over. So far we were tied at one game apiece. Sonja did not like to lose. Neither did I. As we whacked the ball back and forth across the net the points went first one way then the other. I was sweating, but then so was she. And then it was my serve, and all I had to do to win was make her miss.

She stood far back on the court, nice legs apart, racket resting on her shoulder, waiting for my serve. She was wearing a white sleeveless blouse with matching tennis shorts. She looked very tanned against all that white. Her shoulder-length blond hair was in a ponytail. She was very tall with a good figure, pretty—nice, even features—but not so pretty you had to fight a roomful of men when you took it out. I

had only known her a week, but we had been to bed
together from the first day. Other than that, I knew
nothing about her. Well, almost nothing. I knew she
was in Corsica on a Russian passport, and that she
had deliberately picked me up in the Calvi Palace
lounge. I didn't know what she did or why she had
latched onto me, and that bothered me a little.

Now she timed my serve perfectly. The ball came
over the net, bounced once, went high. I ran three
steps to my right, pivoted, and whacked the thing in
what I hoped was a bullet shot that would barely
clear the net. The ball skimmed over. Sonja ran up
quickly and got her racket in the way just before the
ball came down. It bounced high in the air, like a
surfboard just after a wipeout when the waves are
playing with it, came over the net still high. I ran to
it, set myself and my racket. Already Sonja was back-
pedaling: she had a pretty good idea of what I was
up to.

I waited for the ball to come down. Out of the
corner of my eye I saw Sonja far back in the court.
When the ball came down, I just love-tapped it over
the net. It bounced low, Sonja ran for it as hard as
she could, but she wasn't in time. The ball bounced
again and then a third time before she could reach it.

I propped my racket on my shoulder and grinned
at her. "In case you just tuned in, that's my game."

"Oh, shut up!" She turned her back on the net and
me and stalked back to the bench where her towel
was.

I figured I'd let her stew awhile. She was always
like this when she lost a game. In about five minutes
she'd get over it. I guess I could have let her win—

some think that's the gentlemanly thing to do. I think it's a lot of pablum pushed by those out to impress. I play to win no matter what it is. I'm probably as bad a loser as Sonja, but I hope I hide it better than she did.

When I thought she'd had enough time to cool down, I went around the net and walked up to her. "Feel like talking about it, or do you want to kick yourself some more?"

She had the towel covering her face. When she pulled it down, she was smiling. It was weak, but it *was* a smile. "I'm sorry," she said, in a voice I could barely hear. She had nice teeth, a little large, and gray-blue eyes with little flecks of gold in them. Her skin was the color of peaches and just as velvety smooth.

"Come on," I said. "I'll buy you a drink." I slid my arm around her slim waist, and we walked the two blocks back to the Calvi Palace.

The lounge was almost deserted. The Corsican bartender grinned a gold smile and twitched a magnificent handlebar moustache. One couple had their heads together in a far booth. Sonja and I made the total present five, counting the bartender.

We sat at a small table, a tired fan circling lazily above us. It wasn't a hot day, but the fan turned anyway. The place had the look of elegance past, a kind of shabby look that showed it was on the downhill slide. The hotel must have been a showplace once, but now there were chips in the scrolled woodwork and the carpeting, which had once been so thick it probably tickled the ankles, was slightly threadbare and leather chairs along the bar had tears in them.

The hotel charged eight dollars a day for room and board. That covered everything but tips—maid service, food and everything else the human body needed. The rooms were as shabby as the lounge but they were clean, and the service was sudden.

The bartender came around the end of the bar and approached us with a practiced smile. He had a towel over his left arm and was carrying a tray. His short red jacket once had gold thread along the lapels, now it looked brassy. His smile showed more gold fillings.

Sonja put her hand on my arm. "Nick, may I have that new drink?" She still had tiny beads of perspiration on her forehead.

"Of course." I looked up at the bartender. "Remember how to make a Harvey Wallbanger?"

The bartender blinked. He wasn't sure. He had made four of them for Sonja the night I introduced them to her.

I said, "It's like an Italian screwdriver, Vodka and orange juice with just a touch of Galiano. But remember, mix the Vodka and orange juice first, then pour just enough Galiano over it to give it a slight film."

He nodded. He remembered now. "Two?" he asked.

"Yes." When he had gone I took Sonja's hand in both of mine. We smiled at each other. "You're a mystery to me, Sonja. I'm trying to figure why, out of all the international handsomes in this lounge that night a week ago, you chose me."

The gray-blue eyes searched my face. The little flecks of gold seemed to sparkle like stars. "Perhaps

you were the handsomest of all," she said softly. She
had a nice voice, low and a little husky.

And that was the problem. I was beginning to like
her; in fact, it was becoming more than "like."

"So we play tennis, lie on the beach, swim, go for
walks—"

"And make love." She squeezed my hand. "We
make love at least twice, sometimes three times every
day, do we not?"

"Yes, that we do. And it seems to get better."

"Then what is wrong?"

"I don't know anything about you . . . who you are,
what you do, why you're here?"

"Is it so important? My darling, Nick, what do I
know about you? Have I asked questions of you?"

"No, you haven't."

"Then why discuss it? We enjoy each other. My
body excites yours and yours, mine. We find pleasure
with each other. Let us not complicate it with . . .
questions."

The bartender came with the drinks in tall frosty
glasses. I paid him and was generous with the tip. His
gold-studded smile broadened. When he was gone, I
lifted my glass to Sonja. "Here's to intrigue and mystery."

She moved her head closer and touched her glass
to mine. Softly she said, "We will drink, then we will
go to your room. We will bathe together, then we will
make love." And she pressed her bare thigh against
mine.

I dropped my hand from the table to her leg. She
pressed a soft breast against my shoulder. We stayed
like that while we drank our Harvey Wallbangers.

And that was exactly what we did. We had the one drink then walked arm in arm, carrying our tennis rackets, to the elevator. Her room was three doors down from mine. We stopped there just long enough for her to deposit her tennis racket and grab a robe. Then we went down to my room.

There were no showers—there usually aren't in the older European hotels. The bath in my room was one of those ornate things that sit on what look like the feet of some kind of animal. They made the tub look like some kind of creature from the deep.

But we did our thing, Sonja and I. While she undressed I got the water running, tested it to the right temperature. I filled the tub halfful, then opened the door to the bedroom so I could undress.

I surprised Sonja. She had just stepped out of her panties, the last thing she still had on. She spun around, those gray-blue eyes wide in surprise. Then the hint of a smile worked on the corners of her mouth. She stood up and posed for me, one leg slightly in front of the other.

She had the ripe, rich body which is completely out of style today when the best women are supposed to be thin and rich. Sonja's richness was in the treasure of her curves. There was a definite roundness to the hips, without a trace of bone. The breasts were large yet firm, young. She was high-waisted and long-legged, which made her legs look thinner than they were. Actually they were as rich and ripe as the rest of her body.

"Is the water ready?" she asked.

"Ready," I said. I waited at the bathroom door for her. She walked purposefully, her breasts barely jiggling with each step. I was standing sideways in the doorway. Sonja stopped, blinked at me in what was supposed to be a look of innocence. "How will I get through, darling? How can I get into the bathroom?"

I gave her a wicked grin, clucked my tongue at her. "Guess you'll just have to try to squeeze through."

She kept the wide-eyed innocent look. "You mean, you won't move?"

"I may be crazy," I said, "but I'm not stupid."

She smiled at me. She made a large thing of it. First she tried to come through front first. That didn't work. You can bet that didn't work. I wasn't about to let that work.

"I guess there is only one way I can get through."

"I guess so."

She turned sideways facing me and started to push slowly past me. Her body slowly melted against mine as she moved directly in front of me. Then her arms went around my neck. "You're still dressed," she said.

"Give me two-tenths of a second."

The girlish innocent look suddenly left those gold-speckled eyes. The smile disappeared. "You *do* like me, don't you?"

With one finger, I tilted her chin up and kissed her on the mouth. "Yes, I like you."

"And you like my body?"

I shrugged. "Not too bad. I've seen worse."

She struck my chest twice with her fists then pushed herself past me into the bathroom. As she started to lift a leg to step into the tub I smacked her one on the fanny. She squealed.

I was half-undressed already. It didn't take long to

finish. The clothes lay right where I took them off. I took two steps which put me right beside the tub, stood there twirling the ends of an invisible moustache. "And now, my pet, alone at last."

Sonja, playing along, hunched forward trying to cover herself with her arms. "What do you intend to do, sir?" she asked timidly.

"Rape and pillage," I grunted and stepped into the tub.

She shrugged and sighed and threw her arms out. "You American men are all alike. Very well. Do with me what you will."

I sat in the water facing her. The tub was so small our legs got all tangled. Sonja was looking at me. There was no innocence in her eyes now. I was looking at her. I moved slightly toward her taking both hands in mine. I pulled her toward me. Then I bent forward and cupped her breasts and kissed them.

"Oh, Nick," she moaned. "I thought we were going to wait until after our bath. I was afraid we would have to wait."

I felt her hand on my leg moving up. My hands went around her waist. I moved them down slightly and moved her up into my lap. She tilted her head back and pulled off the band tying back her long blond hair. Then her cheek pressed against mine and the downy hair tickled my shoulder. I pulled her closer.

I felt her breath on my ear, growing quicker and warmer. Her hands stroked the back of my neck as I stroked her.

Suddenly I said, "I wonder if this tub is an antique?

Could be eighteenth century ... do you know anything about antiques?"

"Nick, will you shut up about this tub!" Her voice had a desperate tone. She raised her knees slightly and moved even closer to me. "Tell me what you really think of my body. Tell me what it does to you when you watch us together. I know you watch." Her arms wrapped tightly around my neck. "Oh, Nick, what are you *doing* to me?"

I smiled slightly. Her body excited me beyond belief, especially when she kept moving it around as she was doing now, moving with anxious excitement.

And I said, "There was a movie floating around the states recently called, the Virgin and the Gypsy. It was about a minister's daughter who gets tangled up with some roving gypsy, and—"

"For God's sake, Nick. Please!" She tried to force herself close enough, but I held her just far enough away to tease her.

"Anyway," I went on. "The advertisement they used for this film was one of the best I've ever seen. It said that once there was a virgin, the daughter of a minister, who met a gypsy. Her father taught her about God, but the gypsy taught her about Heaven."

Sonja started digging her fingernails into the back of my neck. Her lips touched my ear and I felt the heat of her breath all the way to my toes. I put both my hands on her hip bones, and lifted her slightly. Her breathing suddenly stopped. Her body tensed, waiting, expectant. Slowly, ever so slowly, I eased her down so that I was entering her. Her breath seemed to come out a very little at a time. The farther I entered the more breath she allowed to escape. She let out a low, long groan. Then her arms wrapped tightly around my neck. My face was lost in the silky strands of her hair.

"Nick," she whispered in a voice so soft I barely heard it. When I started to speak she hushed me. "No," she whispered. "Let me finish." She moved slightly and let out another groan. "Listen, darling. It has never been like this for me, not with anyone."

She had gotten to me. I was beginning to move against her.

"Yes," I said through clenched teeth. "Yes, I like your body. Yes, it excites me. Yes, I enjoy making love to it."

Suddenly her fingernails clawed at me. "Oh!" she cried. "Oh! Darling, I can't . . . wait . . . any . . . longer. . . ." She wiggled against me. Her body jerked violently twice, then three times. She made little whimpering sounds like a child. She shivered, almost seemed to go into convulsions, then her arms and legs wrapped themselves around me and her body relaxed as though there were no bones in it. I'd never before known a woman who could give herself so completely to satisfaction.

"My turn," I said. I started moving again.

"No!" she cried. "No, don't move. I don't want you to move."

I leaned back slightly so that she wasn't molded quite so solidly with me.

"Stop looking," she said.

"I enjoy looking. You're easy to look at, especially when we're joined. Now show me how good you really are, before the bath water gets cold."

"If it gets cold I'll warm it again." She started moving again, slowly at first. Her lips came to my ear. "Nick," she whispered. "Nick, what we have is so much better than good. It is so much better than anything."

I was losing myself to her and I knew it. I was moving out of myself, my soul and mind were both leaving. I was caught up in the magic of what she was doing. Parts of me were leaving my body. It was building and I didn't want it to stop.

My head exploded like a tin can with a firecracker inside. The rest of my body followed. I came unglued like a cheap puzzle. Bells rang loudly in my head. I couldn't stop them. There were church bells, fire bells, all kinds of bells. Time zipped by in flashes like the speed of light.

And then suddenly Sonja pulled away from me. She had moved that magnificent body and pushed away from me. There was a woosh of air where her body had been. I suddenly felt very cold.

"Nick," Sonja said. "Someone is at the door. Oh, Nick, it is a rotten trick, but someone is ringing the doorbell."

I snapped to quickly. The bell rang again, an ancient chime from a more elegant era. I studied Sonja's flushed cheeks closely. "Did you. . . ?"

She nodded. "Yes, darling. With you. Toss me my robe as you go out, will you?"

I pushed myself up and padded out. At the bathroom door, I grabbed Sonja's robe and tossed it toward her. Then I slipped into my own robe and opened the door.

A small, dark boy smiled up at me. He needed a haircut but his brown, intense eyes looked intelligent. They also looked about five years older than the boy himself.

"Signor Neek Carter?" he asked in a voice that revealed his age.

"That's me."

"Telegram." He produced a dirty tin tray with the familiar Western Union yellow on it. Only, there were two telegrams.

I selected the top one. "Thank you," I took a half-dollar from the dresser top and handed it to him.

He waited. He blinked his young-old eyes and studied my earlobe.

Then I got the message. "Who is the other telegram for?" I asked.

He flashed me a huge, perfectly white smile. "For thee Signorina. Shee ees not in her room."

"I'll take it." I gave him another half-dollar and whacked him on the rear as he took off down the hall.

Sonja came out of the bathroom, tying her robe. The ends of her hair were wet. I gave her telegram to her and opened my own. Mine was short and sweet. It was from Hawk. He wanted me in Washington immediately.

I looked at Sonja as she read hers. Then something she had said came back to me. Something about if anything happened. . . . I shook it off. It was probably nothing. I waited until she had finished reading her telegram, then I said, "I hope yours is better news than mine."

She blinked at me. "I have been expecting it."

"You have to go back to Russia?"

"No," she said, shaking her head. "It is from a man called Mr. Hawk. I am to report immediately to the headquarters of AXE in Washington, D. C. . ."

TWO

It was snowing in Washington as the taxi pulled up in front of the Amalgamated Press and Wire Services on Dupont Circle. I got out and pulled the collar of my overcoat up around my neck. An icy wind slapped my face. It was a long way from Corsica.

I reached back into the cab to help Sonja out. She was wearing a heavy suede coat with a fox collar. She took my hand, stepped out of the cab and stood with shoulders hunched against the wind-blown snow as I paid the driver.

I knew now exactly as much as I did the day we received the telegrams. Nothing. All the questions I had leveled at her had been met by a shaking head and deaf ears. On the plane, she had been quiet and moody.

Then, just before we landed in Washington, she had touched my arm lightly. "Nick," she said softly. "I meant what I said about it being better with you than anyone else. I want you to know that. We have a wonderful relationship and I want to keep it as long as I can. Please don't ask me any more questions. You will learn what you need to know soon."

So I became silent too. But the questions remained.

19

Sonja moved about on a Russian passport. Was she a Soviet agent? If so, what was she doing in Corsica? And why would Hawk summon her as well as me? Hawk had to know she was with me, that meant Hawk knew who she was, what she was doing. Sure, all I had to do was wait until we saw Hawk. But I didn't like the way I had been suckered.

I took Sonja's arm and we climbed the steps to the main entrance. The day was gloomy, depressing. Heavy gray snow clouds hovered low, and the wind was so cold it seemed unbearable. Yes, indeed, I was a long, long way from Corsica.

When we got inside we stood in the hallway for a minute, letting the warmth of the building soak through. I shook snow from the shoulders of my overcoat and put the collar down. Then, taking Sonja's arm, I pointed the way to Hawk's office.

He was in shirt sleeves behind his desk when we went in. There were papers scattered all over. In one liquid quick movement Hawk came out of his chair and around the desk, grabbing up his jacket and shrugging into it. It hung loosely on his spare frame. His leathery face crinkled into a smile as he approached Sonja. Only the eyes showed the strain of his job. Taking the stub of a cigar out of his mouth, he straightened his tie and offered Sonja his hand.

"Good of you to come, Miss Treshenko," he said. Then he looked at me and nodded. "I imagine you have quite a few questions, right, Carter?"

"One or two, yes, sir."

Hawk waved a hand toward two chairs on this side of his desk. "Sit down both of you, please." He went

around the desk and took his own squeaky chair. It
was warm in the office.

Sonja and I sat down and waited patiently while
Hawk crackled cellophane paper from a fresh, black
cigar. I knew it would do no good for me to start
asking a lot of questions. Hawk had a way about him,
a flair for the dramatic. It was one of his two major
personality quirks; the other was an almost fervent
love of gadgetry and gimmicks.

He sat across from us now playing a lighted match
over the end of the cigar. The room was soon dotted
with cloudy puffs of smelly cigar smoke. I saw Sonja's
nose wrinkle and I had a rough time trying to keep
from smiling.

She was watching Hawk intently, the way a child
watches a spider spin a web or a worm crawl along a
tree branch. It occurred to me that to someone who
didn't know him well, Hawk *would* seem a bit
strange. I could see why Sonja would stare. But Hawk
wasn't strange to me, he was . . . well . . . Hawk.

"Now then," he began. He leaned forward, the
smoking cigar clenched tightly between his teeth.
"Shall we get on with it?" He riffled through the
papers in front of him and pulled three of them out.
He looked up first at Sonja, then at me. "AXE has
never had anything dumped in its lap with so little to
go on. Frankly, we have next to nothing."

Sonja moved a little forward in her chair. "Sir, I
don't want to interrupt, but I'm sure Nick doesn't
think I should be here. If you could explain—"

"All in good time, Miss Treshenko." Hawk turned to
me. "Miss Treshenko was sent to Corsica by me. It
was her request to be paired with the best agent AXE

had, so I told her you were in Corsica. I wanted you two to get to know each other."

"Why?"

"I'll explain that later." He chomped on his cigar, puffed smoke and studied the papers in front of him for a few seconds. Then he looked at us again. "As I said, there is little to go on, damned little. Our radar picked up an object somewhere in the Arctic last week. Search planes went out and found nothing. Then, three days ago, we got the same kind of blip. Again search planes went out. Again nothing. We know something is out there, but we don't know what. It may be something that moves in and out of the Arctic, or it may be something deep under the ice."

Sonja and I exchanged glances. But the look she gave me said she already knew all of this, that it was no surprise to her. I felt like a schoolboy coming into class ten minutes after it has started.

"That isn't all," Hawk went on. He shuffled the papers in his hands, turned the top one over. "Our patrol ships operating north of the Bering Sea have picked up Sonar patterns of subs—nuclear subs. They must be carrying tons of atomic arms. There were four incidents last week. We know subs are there, but they always disappear before we can pinpoint them. The Navy guesses they are dipping under the Arctic ice."

"That's a pretty large guess," I said.

"It's more than a guess." Hawk pushed the button on his intercom.

A female voice came on. "Yes, sir?"

"Alice, will you bring in the world globe, please?"

"Right away, sir."

Hawk clicked off. He looked across the desk at me. The fire had gone out of his cigar, and he just chewed on it. "We have more than a guess, Nick. We sent search planes crisscrossing all over the Bering Sea. On four separate occasions they sighted subs."

I frowned. "Whose subs? From where?"

Hawk pulled the cigar from between his teeth. "Red Chinese subs. They enter the Bering Sea. We keep tabs on them. They suddenly disappear."

"They don't come out?" I asked.

Hawk shook his head. "The first one was sighted over a week ago. It hasn't been seen or heard of since. No, the Navy is right—they go under the Polar ice cap and they stay there."

I said slowly, "Then they must have a destination under there, some activity."

Sonja was silent, but she was following the conversation with interest. There was a light knock, then the door opened. Alice came in carrying a fairly large globe, the kind that turns on a stand.

Alice was a dark-haired woman in her early 50s. She was short with fat legs and a large fanny. She had a mouth the size of a prune and just as smooth, and her voice sounded like a scratched phonograph record. But she had a heart as big as all outdoors and as soft as oatmeal. She had helped me more than once, softening Hawk's anger when I pulled something AXE wouldn't approve of, or getting me information I couldn't get anywhere else. Alice had a beauty you couldn't see. She was my kind of woman.

She set the globe on Hawk's desk, blessed me with a

smile and a wink and left the room as silently as a fly
walking on a wall.

Sonja and I leaned forward. Hawk placed both
hands on the globe.

"I think we can narrow the destination of those
subs a little," he said. "As you both know, it would be
almost impossible to search the entire Arctic Circle to
find out what the Chicoms are up to. Even the blips
on the radar screen covered too wide an area. We
wanted to narrow it and still be close to where those
blips came from. One of our radar men came up with
this idea. Watch."

Hawk pulled out a soft-tipped pencil. He put the
point on Washington, D. C., and drew a red line
north, then all around the globe until he came back to
Washington.

He looked up at us. "Notice I moved the line north.
Always north. Now watch this."

He spun the globe enough to bring Russia in front
of him. He put the point of the pencil on Moscow and
started another line north. He drew it around the
globe and ended back at Moscow. He tilted the
sphere so we could see the top of it. The two lines
crossed in the Arctic Circle.

"The best we can narrow it is an area of about fifty
square miles. Right there." He tapped his finger where
the two lines crossed.

I nodded. "And my assignment is to try and find
out what the Chinese are doing and where they are
doing it."

Hawk nodded. "*And* destroy whatever they're
doing, if you feel it is necessary. We've code-named
this 'Ice Bomb Zero,' after those Arctic subs filled with

nuclear weaponry. From now on, when you communicate with me, refer to it."

I looked over at Sonja as Hawk lit his cigar again. I was beginning to get vibrations about why she was here. I felt I knew what Hawk was going to say next even before he said it. Sonja smiled at me.

Hawk said, "When we found that those two lines connected from Washington and Moscow, we notified the Soviet Union. The Soviets are as anxious as we are to find out what is happening. We have made ... certain arrangements."

I frowned. "What kind of arrangements?"

"You will take a quick survival course which will be given in the Soviet Union."

I blinked at him. "I will *what?*"

Hawk puffed twice. "You won't be in Russia alone. In fact, someone will be taking the course with you and will accompany you on your Arctic search. One of Russia's top agents, I understand."

"Who?" I said, but I didn't really have to ask. Hawk gave a short laugh. "Miss Treshenko, of course. She will be going with you on Ice Bomb Zero."

THREE

I was more than a little leery about taking Sonja into Special Effects and Editing. Now that I knew she was a Soviet agent, the old enemy defense mechanisms were automatically set within me. Enough of them had tried to kill me. But when we were alone, Hawk told me that a particular section of Special Effects and Editing had been set aside for Sonja and I to visit. There was no danger of her seeing something she had no business seeing. We were to meet Dr. Dan Michaels who would give us most of our supplies and would brief us on what to expect from now on.

In the cab on the way over, Sonja surprised me by taking my hand and squeezing it. I looked out the side window. I could feel her eyes on my face. It was as if somebody had a magnifying glass focusing a sunspot on my left cheek. But there was no sun and no magnifying glass, there was only Sonja sitting next to me, holding my hand and staring at me.

I turned and the lovely gray-blue eyes seemed to have gained a million little gold flecks. They smiled at me.

"Are you angry?" she asked.

"You might have told me in Corsica. If I'd known you were a Soviet agent, I would have . . ."

"What? Ignored me? Treated me differently? I didn't want that. We were happy there. We pleased each other. We could still please each other."

"Maybe. But I haven't got the whole picture of who—or what—you are. Several pieces are still missing."

She sighed deeply. She was still wearing the brown suede coat and there was no mistake about there being a woman's body under it. "My government ordered me not to reveal any more than was absolutely necessary. Hawk knew. He could have told you."

"Maybe he thought you would handle that common courtesy yourself since you were coming to Corsica to meet me."

"I *wanted* to meet you. You know, you are quite famous in Moscow. The indestructible Nick Carter. Killmaster. Code name N-3. Do you still have the AXE tattoo on your arm?"

I didn't like this. She knew far too much. "You seem to be well informed, Miss Treshenko."

She leaned over and kissed my cheek. "I wanted to meet you," she said again. "I wanted to see the kind of man no Russian could kill." Long, thick lashes drooped demurely over the gray-blue eyes. "That was at first. After I got to know you and we . . . well, everything was so perfect, so beautiful between us I . . . didn't want to spoil it."

"You seem to know all about me, but I know almost nothing about you, that puts me at a disadvantage."

She brightened the back seat of the cab with her smile. "Do you want to know about me? I was born on Kaluzhskaya Street, close to the banks of the Moscow River. I spent my childhood in the State Conservatory of Music, there in Moscow. I played in Lenin or Gorky Park. I attended Moscow State University, then went into the State Department. I have spent eight years learning the American brand of English. For the past two years, I have been studying the life and habits of one Nicholas Carter. I know you almost as well as you know yourself."

I felt something like a breath of wind brush the hair on the back of my neck. It was as if I stood naked in a room lined with one-way mirrors, and everyone passing by could look in and see my nakedness. "Why?" I asked, in a voice that didn't sound like mine.

Her smile stayed. "Purely personal, darling. I wanted to know all about a man no one could kill. I knew you were a ladies' man, that you were a very good lover. I felt that when I met you, I could go one of two ways. I could refuse at all costs to let you get me into bed and try to keep you interested by teasing you, or I could let you seduce me. When I did meet you I knew at once that 'playing hard to get,' as you say, would not work. You had a great deal of charm, and if you wanted me badly enough I would not be able to stop you—I know my own weaknesses. So, I decided on the alternative, to let you seduce me as soon as possible. That done, there would be no cat-and-mouse about whether we would or wouldn't. I knew it would be good, I didn't think I would be disappointed, but ... I never expected ... I mean, it was so much better than I ... Look at me, blushing like a schoolgirl."

The woman was almost spooky. I felt there wasn't a move I could make without her knowing about it. She had my number, and a couple of things about that bothered me. One, I still didn't have *her* number. And two, now that she had mine, what was she planning to do with it? Yes, I was attracted to her— she was more woman than I had met, or would meet again, in a very long time. Yes, she turned me on. But there was something about her, something I couldn't quite pinpoint. She had a way of looking at me when she talked, a way of making me want to believe every word she said, and yet . . .

"Here we are, sir," the driver said. He pulled the cab to the curb in front of the building.

I wasn't sure if I should take Sonja right inside, or wait for someone to meet us. The decision wasn't left up to me. As I was paying the cab driver, Dr. Michaels came down the steps. He gave a short nod to Sonja, smiled at me and extended his hand.

"Good to see you again, Nick."

"Doctor."

Doctor Michaels was a spare, stoop-shouldered man with rimless glasses and thinning sandy hair. He wore a loose-fitting suit without an overcoat. We shook hands, and I introduced him to Sonja.

"It's a pleasure meeting you, Miss Treshenko," he said politely. He waved his hand toward the building behind him. "Shall we take the side entrance?"

We followed him around the side along a freshly-shoveled sidewalk and down wet cement steps to what appeared to be the basement of the building. The doctor unlocked a solid-looking door, and we

went inside. I had never been to this part of Special
Effects and Editing.

The room we entered was large and bare of furni-
ture. When Doctor Michaels hit the light switch, the
room brightened with a harsh glare. Over in a corner
I noticed equipment and things piled.

"Is that our equipment?" I asked.

"Some of it," the doctor said.

We were standing in the middle of the room. Sonja
was looking around. Her gaze came to rest on a door
leading to another part of the building. She had more
than the curiosity of a woman, she had the curiosity
of a spy.

I touched her arm. "Let's check out what we have
here, Sonja." The doctor and I exchanged glances. We
both knew we shouldn't linger there. It wouldn't be
long before Sonja began asking questions.

She came willingly enough. We crossed to where
the equipment was stashed. It was mostly cold-
weather gear—parkas, fishnet longjohns, heavy boots.
There was some survival stuff, plus skis, tents, sleep-
ing bags.

The doctor came up behind us. "Perhaps Miss Treshenko would prefer to use equipment from her own
country?"

Sonja smiled at him. "Not at all, Doctor." She
glanced past him at that door again.

"How much have you been told about your training,
Nick?" Dr. Michaels asked.

"Just that it would be in Russia."

Sonja moved quietly to another part of the room
where two back packs rested against a wall.

"Here's how it will work," the doctor said. "You will

both take a plane from here to San Francisco then board an American sub going north to the Bering Strait. There you transfer to a Russian vessel which will deliver you to a small, guarded compound just outside the town of Uelen in the Soviet Union. That's where you take the survival course. When it's completed, you'll fly, via Soviet military transport, to an American base camp in the Arctic where you pick up transportation, food, and anything else needed for the mission."

I nodded and looked at Sonja. She had opened one of the back packs and was fishing inside it. The heat in the room was beginning to make me uncomfortable in my heavy overcoat but I kept it on. Underneath I was a walking arsenal. I had Wilhelmina, my stripped Luger, in its holster under my left armpit; Hugo, the thin stiletto, in its sheath along my left arm, ready to drop into my hand at the shrug of a shoulder, and Pierre, the tiny, deadly gas bomb, was taped in the hollow behind my right ankle bone.

"Any questions?" Dr. Michaels asked.

"Yes," Sonja called, straightening up. She motioned toward the back packs. "I believe I would prefer the Soviet brand."

Dr. Michaels nodded. "Whatever you wish, Miss Treshenko." He saw the puzzled look on my face.

"What's in the back packs?" I asked.

"Explosives." Then he blinked. "Didn't Hawk tell you? Miss Treshenko is a demolitions expert."

I shot a look at Sonja. She was smiling at me.

FOUR

Sonja didn't take my hand again until we were on the transport, flying toward San Francisco. The cargo plane was rigged with two large comfortable seats, but we were sitting in uncomfortable silence when Sonja took my hand.

She squeezed it and once again her eyes searched my face. "Nick," she said softly. "Nick, please."

"Please—what?"

"Darling, we are going to be together for a long time. We can't let it stay like this."

"What am I supposed to do? Act like nothing has changed? Are we still in Corsica?"

"No. But we have an assignment. We must complete it together. The least we could do is try to remain friends ... lovers, if you'd like."

"All right. What else do I still have to learn about you? So far you've transformed yourself from a girl I met on Corsica and had some kicks with to a Soviet agent and demolitions expert on assignment with me. How many other little surprises do you have?"

"None, darling. You know it all now. We are both agents, all right, but we are also human beings. We are a man and a woman, and I, the woman, care a great deal for the man. I hope you can return the feeling ... at least a little. It is very important to me."

I turned to look at her. She was watching me anxiously, and the little specks of gold glittered in her eyes. I tilted her chin up slightly with my finger, gently kissed her lips. "Sometimes I can almost believe you," I said. "Almost forget we operate on different sides of the fence." I smiled. "Sometimes."

She countered with, "I wish we weren't on this plane. I wish we were alone ... back in Corsica."

"We'll be alone again." I shifted position in the seat, glanced out of the window. We were flying over the Sierra Nevadas now and, as always, the air was turbulent. I could smell her perfume and, yes, I could almost believe her. Sonja put her head on my shoulder.

But I just couldn't let myself believe her completely. She was a beautiful woman and an affectionate one—a combination few men can put up a defense against. Few would want to. But I couldn't forget she was a Soviet agent, my enemy and the enemy of my country.

So we had to work together, I couldn't help that. There was something odd going on in the Arctic that interested both the Soviet Union and the United States. We had to find out what it was. But ... what if the Soviets had sent a male agent? How would I have felt then? I would probably be waiting for him to try to kill me when my back was turned. The Russians had tried often enough. And maybe they knew that, maybe they knew I would be hostile to a man. Maybe that was why they had sent a woman.

The transport set down at the Alameda Air Station,

just outside San Francisco. It was late and we hadn't eaten since leaving Washington. As we left the plane, we were greeted by the Executive Officer of the Naval Air Base, a young lieutenant commander with a chestful of ribbons. He treated us with official politeness and directed us to a waiting Cadillac. I saw the officers standing around the plane eyeing Sonja's legs as she walked from the plane to the car. If they had any comments, they kept them to themselves. The enlisted men weren't hampered by protocol. There was a wolf whistle or two and a lot of growling. Sonja simply smiled with the confidence of a woman who knows exactly what she has.

We were driven to the Officers Club and a rich buffet. While we ate, Sonja spent a great deal of time smiling at the officers around us. She wasn't the only woman there, but she was far and away the most attractive, and she knew it.

We were seated next to each other at a long table. The officers were introduced as staff of the submarine we would be boarding. The skipper was a young man, a few years younger than the base Executive Officer, also a Lieutenant-commander.

There was a good deal of joking and laughter around the table. Sonja was obviously enjoying herself. The officers treated her with a friendly respect. They kidded her a little about making sure all secret plans were locked up tight before she boarded. And she delighted them by saying she had no idea American Naval Officers were so young and handsome. Surely, the Soviet Union should take a lesson in recruitment.

Her humor and outgoing manner matched theirs.

She might be a Soviet agent, but that night she won the heart of every man around that table. And maybe a little more of mine.

After the buffet, we were separated. I didn't see Sonja again until the next morning when we boarded the sub.

It was a misty, San Francisco day. The gray sky seemed low enough to touch, and the landing strips shone with wetness. I had heard at breakfast that all flight operations had been postponed until afternoon.

I was walking with the skipper of the sub across wet asphalt to where the sub was moored. I could see plenty of activity on deck, and I wondered where Sonja was. I had no idea where she had spent the night.

The skipper's name was Nielson. He saw me check the sub from one end to the other and then look all around us and caught on immediately.

"She's all right," he said, taking out a well-used pipe and some matches.

I smiled at him. "I'm sure she is—by the way, what do I call you? Commander? Skipper?"

He chuckled as he worked a match over the pipe bowl.

"Mr. Carter, in the Navy the man in charge of any ship is always addressed as Captain. It doesn't matter whether he's a full captain, a lieutenant, or a petty officer, he's still captain." He smiled, the stem of the pipe clenched between his teeth. "I'm not saying that to sound superior, I just want you to feel comfortable while you're aboard."

I nodded. "Well, I want to thank you, and your

men, Captain, for the fine treatment you gave Miss Treshenko last night."

He smiled. "Don't mention it, Mr. Carter."

I cleared my throat. "Would I be stepping out of line if I asked where she spent the night? I mean, I do feel a little responsible for her."

The skipper chuckled. "You're not out of line. She spent the night at my house."

"I see."

"I don't think so. She stayed with me, my wife, and our four brats. She seemed to take to the kids. I guess they took to her too. She's quite a gal."

"So I'm beginning to find out."

We had reached the ramp leading to the sub. Nielson was piped aboard. He saluted the flag flying astern, then the officer of the day.

I said to the officer of the day, "Request permission to come aboard."

"Granted," he answered.

I stepped aboard the slippery deck, feeling out of place in a business suit and rain coat. Men in dungarees moved about coiling lines. Captain Nielson led the way down a ladder and along a narrow passageway to the officer's mess. Sonja was there, sipping coffee.

She gave me a big smile as I stepped in. There were three officers sitting around her. She was wearing dungarees, just like the enlisted men I had seen topside, only she did more for them.

One of the officers at the table turned to Nielson. "Mike, where are you going to put this lovely creature?"

The skipper grinned. We were getting ourselves

coffee. "In my personal quarters," he said, "but I think I'll bunk in with you."

The other two officers laughed. The one who had spoken to Nielson said, "I've been trying to convince Miss Treshenko she should at least *try* to get some military secrets out of me."

"You gentlemen have all been so very nice," Sonja said.

Nielson and I sat at the table. A bugle sounded over the loudspeaker, announcing to the enlisted men to come and get their chow. I checked my watch. It was a little after six.

"We'll be shoving off at oh-nine-hundred," Captain Nielson said.

I looked at Sonja's smiling face. "You don't look so bad early in the morning."

She lowered her long eyelashes mockingly. "Thank you."

"Enjoying yourself?"

"Completely."

I didn't get a chance to talk to her alone until later that afternoon, after we had passed under the Golden Gate and were well out to sea.

The sub was traveling on the surface; it would not submerge until we were close to the Bering Strait. I donned my overcoat and went up on deck. The fog was gone. There was an icy chill in the air but the sea looked the clearest blue I had ever seen. Its luster was matched only by the bright blueness of the sky. The sun was shining; the air felt pure. I donned my overcoat and stood close to the bow holding the rail lines for support. The sea wasn't rough but there was a chop. Whitecaps jumped all around.

I was smoking a cigarette, watching the bow dip and rise, when Sonja came and stood beside me.

"Hello, stranger," she said lightly. "I know you from somewhere, don't I?"

I turned to look at her. The wind had caught her blond hair and was whipping it around her face in cobweblike strands. She still wore the dungarees and had added a pea jacket that was way too large. The cold and the wind gave a glowing red blush to her cheeks.

I smiled at her. "You're the most popular person on board."

There was no answering smile on her lips. "I want to touch you," she said simply.

"Now, how would that look to the officers and men of this vessel?"

"I don't give a damn how it would look." The golden flecks in her eyes sparked and multiplied. "I want to be alone with you. I want to touch you and I want you to touch me."

I moved closer to her. "I don't know when we'll be alone again. There are five officers and twenty-three men aboard this sub. It's a small vessel. I doubt if we'll ever be more alone than we are now."

"Hold my hand, Nick," she said. "At least do that."

I sighed and kept both hands in the pockets of my overcoat. "You're teasing me, Sonja, and you know it. I'm beginning to think all this attention has gone to your head."

She stood away from me and looked at me curiously, her head cocked a little to the right. The outsize pea jacket made her look like a little girl.

"You are a little puzzling, Nick. You're much too

handsome for your own good, you know I suppose it is the way of American men. All these officers, they are so young and handsome . . . and so boyish almost. But you, you are not boyish at all."

I frowned at her. "It sounds like you've been studying me again."

She nodded. "Perhaps. I am curious to know why no agent has ever succeeded in assassinating you. Surely some have come close. All communist agents cannot be bumbling fools. How many attempts have been made on your life?"

"I don't keep count. But then I'm not interested in the failures. I'd be very interested in any successful attempt."

I flipped my cigarette into the sea. "This is a little off the subject, isn't it? I thought we were talking about how we're going to get to be alone."

She smiled at me. "I will find a way. When we are in Russia, I will definitely find a way."

There was no way as long as we were on that sub. For the next two days, every time I saw Sonja she was surrounded by men. We ate with Captain Nielson and the rest of the officers, and although we spent a great deal of time together we were never alone. There were always men around her, and she basked in their admiration. And, being totally female, she teased me whenever she could, knowing my hands were tied.

Off the coast of Alaska, the sub finally submerged. The weather had turned bitterly cold. Even my overcoat wasn't quite warm enough. The officers and men were issued longjohns, and so were Sonja and I.

On the night of our fourth day at sea we made

radio contact with the Russian trawler. A rendezvous point was arranged. Sonja and I would board the trawler the next morning. I thought I detected a look of sadness in Sonja's eyes when she heard the news. When I and two officers escorted her to chow, she seemed unusually quiet.

The officers joked with her as usual as we ate. Captain Nielson remarked that the pea jacket she had been wearing would never fit the sailor who owned it quite the same again. But Sonja's response was somehow half-hearted.

After the meal a cake was brought in. Written across the top of it was "Good Luck, Sonja." When she saw that, her lower lip quivered a little. Then something else happened.

As she was cutting the cake, a Chief Petty Officer appeared at the door with a gift from the enlisted men. Sonja sat for a long time just silently staring at the package. Finally, as the officers kept prompting her, she opened the thing. It was a ring, perfectly fitted for her in the size I had given the men. It had a miniature picture of the sub on the face and had been turned on a machine shop lathe from gold provided by the sub's dentist.

Sonja put it on the ring finger of her right hand.

"There's an inscription," Captain Nielson said. All the officers were smiling at her.

She pulled the ring off and read the inscription. I had already read it. It was signed with affection from the crew of the sub. Sonja gave a little sob and pushed her chair back. Then she was up and running from the room.

It was strangely quiet after she had gone. We all

sat around the table looking at half-empty coffee cups. It was Captain Nielson who broke the silence.

"Women are very emotional about things like that," he said.

The rest of us nodded or murmured agreement and sipped our coffee. The next morning, when Sonja and I boarded the Russian trawler, she was wearing the ring.

The rendezvous was almost at the exact line dividing the United States from Russia. We surfaced in the Bering Strait and waited for the trawler to come alongside.

It was so cold it was unbelievable. Ice floes drifted by. I no longer wore a business suit and overcoat; I had a Navy issue parka and thermal underwear. But I still carried my little "arsenal" on me.

The Russian trawler was taking her time reaching us, the bow cutting through ice just to our port. Sonja and I were waiting on deck, watching.

There was tension aboard the sub. Captain Nielson stood on the bridge watching through binoculars. He watched not only the trawler but the sea around it. The sub gunners were at their stations.

My eyebrows and eyelashes were dusted with frost. I tried to snuggle down deeper into the parka hood. I shot a glance at Sonja, but all I could see of her face was the tip of her nose. It was becoming increasingly difficult for me to breathe through my own nose. When I reached up with my mitten-covered hand, I was surprised to find my nostrils plugged with ice.

The trawler came alongside, its powerful diesels turning in reverse. I watched as lines were thrown and caught. Once both vessels were locked together,

the Russian captain looked across from his bridge at
Captain Nielson, his face set hard. The sub's skipper
matched the look.

If that was a fishing trawler, it went after very
large fish with some very unusual equipment. There
was a machine gun mounted on the bow that looked
to be at least fifty caliber. On a high mast a radar
screen turned constantly. Every crewman standing on
deck was armed with a rifle.

Suddenly the Russian captain did something totally
unexpected. He saluted Captain Nielson. The salute
was immediately returned. A plank was lowered connecting the sub with the trawler.

For an instant, as I took Sonja's arm and we walked
to the plank, my eyes locked with the Russian captain's. The look I saw in his was enough to make me
pause. If I had been alone, or if I had been running, I
would have reached for Wilhelmina. It was a look
you killed before it killed you. I had seen it before ...
and I knew I would not be welcome on board that
trawler.

Two of the Russian crewmen reached out to help
Sonja as she stepped from the plank to the trawler.
The sea was rough and a dismal grey. The chunks of
ice that bounced by were the color of fresh-cut flesh,
the stark white that shows an instant before the blood
begins to flow.

The crewmen took Sonja by the elbows and helped
her aboard. Then it was my turn. I stepped gingerly
along the plank. As I neared the trawler, I saw, out of
the corner of my eye, the Russian captain step out
from the bridge to look down at me.

The crewmen waiting for me glanced up for just an

instant. But in that instant the captain gave them a
message, an order. I stood on the wobbling plank and
looked up. Again the captain and I locked eyes.

The message he had given his crewmen was simple. I wouldn't last twenty seconds in that icy sea. If I
happened to slip off the plank, the captain would not
have to deal with the foolishness of transporting
American agents to Russia.

He looked down at me. He wasn't a particularly tall
man, less than five-eleven, but he projected strength.
He had a massive build, his parka extended his shoulders to the point where he almost looked like he was
wearing football pads. But I didn't see his strength as
massive. I saw it as primitive, basic, as basic as the
design of an axe.

He stood looking down on me from his pitching
perch. Although the ship rocked, he seemed to stand
perfectly still, his hands shoved deep into the pockets
of his parka.

The plank was becoming difficult to stand on. I
had no intention of going for a swim in that icy,
killing water and moved quickly toward the trawler.
Sonja had already been taken below.

The two crewmen watched me come, their rifles
slung over their shoulders on slings. The plank was
slippery, but not as slippery as the bobbing deck of
the trawler. They watched me as I reached the ship.
One of them almost leaned forward to help me, but
then they both fell back. A wave sloshed up between
the trawler and sub. It threw me off balance. I
weaved back and forth on the plank, one foot almost
poised to step aboard the trawler. The two Russian
sailors watched me without expression. The entire

crew was watching but no one moved to help me. The trawler pitched, and to keep from going over, I dropped to one knee.

I slapped my hands flat, palms down on the plank. Sea spray soaked me and wet down the plank. Gritting my teeth, I got back to my feet and stepped quickly to the deck of the trawler.

Once on deck I grabbed a hand rail for support. I was so damned mad I couldn't have spoken to any of them without creating an international incident. But I stood and stared with open hatred at the two crewmen. For awhile they matched my stare. Then they looked down and away. The pair moved off. I looked up at the bridge, but the captain was gone.

My pants and parka were wet and beginning to freeze.

I turned to go below and saw Sonja. She had come back on deck and must have seen what happened. There was a look on her face I had never seen there before, a look of complete disgust.

Then the distance between us was suddenly closed. She came to me and wrapped her arms around my waist. "I am sorry!" she cried. "Oh, Nick, I am so sorry." She leaned back to look up at me. "Please forgive the crude, piggish manners of my countrymen. You can rest assured this little incident will be reported. When I am finished, the captain of this ship will have trouble giving orders on a rowboat."

I looked back across the gap between the trawler and the sub. The plank had been pulled in and the two vessels were drifting apart. I saw Captain Nielson near the sub's conning tower. He looked at us and gave a short salute. I was sorry to see him go . . .

The trawler spent the rest of the day moving slowly through the ice-dotted water. I had changed into dry clothes and Sonja had fixed me a cup of Russian tea, which wasn't half-bad. I could sense the hostility of the crew whenever I came into contact with any of them, but there were no further incidents—not until we reached Uelen.

It was dark when the trawler docked. Two crewmen jumped ashore with lines to make her fast. A plank was lowered but this time there was no pitching sea. The same two crewmen were stationed at the plank. Sonja went ahead of me as before and they helped her along. Evidently she had had a few words with the captain because when I started for the plank the men reached out to help me too. I slapped their hands away and I walked the plank without any help from them. Bad public relations but what the hell—I was mad.

There were four men waiting on the dock, dressed in heavy overcoats. They greeted Sonja warmly, shook my hand and welcomed me to the Soviet Union. Sonja took my arm and guided me back to one of the men.

"Nick, this is Dr. Perska. He will be our instructor for the next three days."

Dr. Perska was a man in his middle 60s, with a craggy, weather-worn face and a magnificent, tobacco-stained handlebar moustache. He spoke no English, but my Russian was not that rusty.

"It is our hope, Mr. Carter," he said in a gravelly voice, "that you will be properly impressed with the course."

"I'm sure I will, doctor."

He smiled, showing gold-capped teeth. "But you are tired. We will begin in the morning. Now you must rest."

He waved his arm, indicating a path leading toward a group of buildings. Sonja fell into step beside me as we walked behind the doctor. The rest of the group were behind us.

I jerked a thumb over my shoulder. "I think we're being followed," I said.

"You should speak Russian, Nick. They will think we are trying to say things we don't want them to hear."

"Okay, so who are they?"

"Security guards. They are here to make sure that ... no one disturbs us."

"Or that I don't try to escape?"

"Nick, you seem very hostile."

"Do I? I wonder why? I certainly don't have any reason to, do I?"

We walked on in silence. I could see the compound ahead now. It was well-guarded—I counted at least five uniformed soldiers. There was a seven-foot wire fence topped with barbed wire. The compound sat on a bluff overlooking the sea. Lights were positioned at each corner of the fence. Large guns faced the sea at the edge of the bluff. Inside the fence were light buildings in two rows of four.

I didn't like it. I didn't like any of it. I wondered why Hawk had let me get into a position like this. I was in a hostile land, surrounded by hostile people, working with an enemy agent.

The guards nodded to us as we stepped inside the

compound. The gate was closed and locked behind us.

Dr. Perska saw me watching. "That is for our own protection, Mr. Carter," he said, with a reassuring smile.

Sonja hugged my arm. "Don't look so glum, darling. We're really not monsters. In fact, we can be very ... nice at times."

Dr. Perska pointed to one of the smaller buildings. "Those are your quarters, Mr. Carter. I hope you will find them comfortable. Miss Treshenko, if you will come with me please."

They walked on and I headed for the building Dr. Perska had indicated. It was little more than a cabin, one room with a fireplace and a connecting bathroom. The carpet looked as though it had been lifted from an old movie theatre. But the fireplace gave the room a cozy warmth. It was a grand fireplace, taking up almost all of one wall.

It was a fireplace you could cuddle up in front of with a friend, one you could picnic in front of, one you could stare into and have deep thoughts about the world situation. It was made of stone and its wood fire crackled. Besides the fireplace there was a double bed with a heavy quilt, and there was a chair and a dresser. My luggage sat in the middle of the room waiting for me. I suddenly realized I *was* tired.

I have to give the Russians credit. They didn't send anyone to kill me until I was almost asleep.

FIVE

When you've been through a day like I'd been through, you just sort of figure something to happen. I went to bed with Wilhelmina close by and I slept, but it was a light sleep.

I don't know what time it was. The fire had died to glowing embers that snapped and popped now and then, and the smell of burning wood filled the room. He opened the door carefully with a key and enough skill to avoid any telltale click. He came in, knife first, and brought a sigh of cold air with him. The door closed behind him without a sound.

He wasn't very tall, and suddenly I realized who it was. The smell of the trawler was still with him.

My eyes just barely open, I watched him come toward the bed. His large bulk glowed in the dying firelight. I had my hand wrapped comfortably around Wilhelmina, finger on the trigger. The stripped Luger lay beside me, outside the quilt by my leg.

He tiptoed, never taking his eyes off the bed. The knife, long and thin, was held against his chest. As he came closer, he raised the knife slightly. I could smell him even better now. That trawler really did do some fishing.

He stopped next to the bed, raised the knife high for the thrust, sucked in his breath. Moving quickly, I raised the business end of the Luger and shoved it just under his nose. In Russian, I said, "If you value your life, let the knife fall behind you."

He was still holding his breath. He hesitated, undecided, his eyes watching my face. If I pulled Wilhelmina's trigger at that range, I'd blow half his head off. He stood motionless, his bulk almost blocking out the fireplace.

It was very warm in that room. There was just enough light from the fire for me to see the beads of sweat on his forehead. The arm holding the knife moved toward me just a little. My finger tightened on the trigger of the Luger. I could kill him easily, and he knew it.

But he tried anyway. His left hand came up quickly, knocked the barrel of the Luger away from his nose. The right hand, holding the knife, came swinging down.

I fired. The explosion seemed to pound against the walls of the room. A section of wall splintered. As I fired, I rolled into him. The knife plunged down toward the mattress.

I hit his knees with my shoulder and kept driving into him. He stumbled back toward the fireplace, the knife still in his hand. I grabbed the edge of the quilt and flapped it over him. He tried to deflect it with his free hand, but it was too big and too heavy. He started clawing at it, but by that time I was off the bed and across the room after him.

As he pulled the quilt down from his face, I rapped the Luger against his nose. He let out a grunt. The knife dropped to the threadbare carpet when he reached up toward what was left of the nose. I brought the Luger down hard on the top of his head. He sank to his knees, his hands to his face.

He hadn't locked the door when he came in. Now it slammed open. Two soldiers were first, holding their rifles at the ready. I already had the Luger on them. Behind them came Doctor Perska, and Sonja.

The trawler captain was still on his knees, making a strange gurgling sound. I bent and picked up the knife. I tossed it to one of the soldiers, and he almost dropped his rifle catching it.

Dr. Perska said, "I heard a shot. I thought. . . ." He was dressed in a heavy robe and high boots. His steel-colored hair was mussed.

"Are you all right, Nick?" Sonja asked. She was also wearing a heavy robe. From the way it draped in front, I knew she was wearing very little under it.

I faced them, looking grand in my longjohns. The two soldiers were helping the trawler captain to his feet. "He tried to kill me," I said.

"You can't be serious," Dr. Perska said.

The soldiers were helping the captain out of the room. I leaned back against the bed. I said, in Russian, "I am speaking in your language so there will be nothing lost in translation. I want no misunderstanding of what I am about to say. I am here under orders from my government. I do not wish to be here. There is not one person here I trust. So, I will put this simply. The next person who tries to come through that door uninvited will be dead before the door closes. I will not ask who it is or why they are here. I will simply kill them."

Dr. Perska looked as if he had just swallowed a bee. "I can't believe an attempt was made on your life, Mr. Carter. Please accept my apologies."

"Offer your apologies again in the morning, doctor. I am not accepting them tonight."

Sonja had been watching me closely. Now she said, "What *will* you accept, Nick?"

"Nothing." I nodded toward the door where the captain had just been taken out. "So what happens to him?"

"He will be sent to Moscow," Sonja said. "He will stand trial there."

"I'm sure he will."

"You do not believe me? Would you like to kill him yourself?"

"If I had wanted to kill him, I would have." I dropped Wilhelmina on the bed. "Now, if you will both please leave, I am going to try to get some sleep. Goodnight."

I turned my back on them and crossed to the dresser where I'd left my special, gold-tipped cigarettes.

I felt a blast of cold air as the door opened and then closed, loudly. The cabin was strangely silent, the only light the red glow from the fireplace. I shook a cigarette out of the box and put it between my lips. Then I remembered I had left my lighter on the bed. I turned ... and saw Sonja.

She stood in front of me holding the lighter. She struck the flame, held it to my cigarette. As I inhaled, I noticed she had unfastened her robe and let it fall open. Underneath, she wore a very sheer, very short powder blue nightie.

I said, "The Luger was on the bed next to the lighter. Why didn't you pick it up instead?"

"Do you really think I want to kill you, Nick? Do you distrust me that much?"

"What *do* you want, Sonja?"

She moved slightly. The robe slid to the edge of her shoulders, then to the floor. "I want your trust, Nick," she said huskily. "But tonight I want more, much more."

Her hands reached for me, slipped behind my neck and pulled my head down. Her soft, moist lips gently brushed the tip of my chin, then moved lightly over each cheek. She took her time tracing the edges of my lips with hers, then let the sweetness of her mouth cover mine. She pressed her body against mine until we were molded together.

She drew back from me. Slowly she took the cigarette from my hand and threw it into the fireplace. She held onto my hand, raised it to her lips and kissed each knuckle. Her tongue darted lightly between each finger. Next she took the hand, turned the palm toward her body, and pressed it to her breast.

I could feel passion rising in me. "You know all the tricks a woman is supposed to know," I said.

"And you?" she murmured. "What tricks do you know?"

I bent slightly and swooped her up in my arms. Her hands locked around my neck. I carried her to the bed and gently placed her there. I put the Luger on the dresser and picked up the quilt from the floor. When I turned back to the bed, Sonja had pulled off her nightgown. She lay there naked sliding her feet slowly up and down against the sheet.

I dropped the quilt across the foot of the bed. "It's going to get very cold tonight," I said.

"I don't think so," she answered, holding out her arms to me.

I always figured longjohns would be difficult to get out of. I don't even remember how I got out of them. All of a sudden I was there with her, holding her in my arms, my lips moving softly against hers.

"Oh, Nick," she whispered. "It's been too long, just too damned long! I've missed you. I've missed your touch. I've missed everything about you."

"Hush."

"Don't wait too long. Promise me you won't."

I didn't.

I felt her stiffen as I moved over her. Her hands were on my shoulders. And when I moved between her legs and entered her, I heard her gasp. She made little whimpering sounds and wrapped her arms and legs tightly around me. And then nothing else meant anything—not the attempt on my life, not whatever was happening in the Arctic. There was nothing outside that cabin, nothing else but that bed, no other woman but her. Sonja had that power, that consuming talent. I was only aware of the perfection of her body. When at last we climbed together to completion, each of us using the other, I was not even aware of myself.

I came back slowly from wherever I had gone. I didn't realize that I was high above her, my arms stiff. She had raised herself to meet me with her arms around my neck. Now she fell back, tongue flicking quickly over her dry lips, eyes closed, moving her head from side to side.

"Oh, Nick, that was so very . . . very. . . ."

"Hush." I started moving against her.

"No," she whimpered. "No more."

"I said hush."

Eyes closed she gave me a dreamy smile. "Yes . . . whatever you say. How can you doubt me now? How can you not trust me?"

I kissed her, moved my hands over the rich curves of her body and enjoyed the total pleasure of making love to her . . . but I could not bring myself to trust her.

We began our course early the next morning. First we had breakfast in a communal hall with all the guards and gun crews and everybody connected with the compound. Every one of them found it necessary to apologize for the attempt on my life the night before. I was assured by all that the trawler captain would be justly dealt with. Somehow I didn't doubt that, but I wondered if it would be because he had tried to kill me . . . or because he had failed to kill me.

Dr. Perska came to sit beside me. His craggy, mustached face was lined with fatigue and anxiety. "Mr. Carter," he said, "you simply *must* accept my apology for last night. I have not slept. I am shocked that such a thing could happen *here*, right under our very noses."

"Don't let it worry you, doctor. Just remember what I told you last night. This course is supposed to last three days, right? You are looking at a very careful man. I intend to stay careful every second I'm here.

All I want you to do is impress me with this survival course."

That he did.

Most of what Sonja and I learned had to do with how we would survive if all our equipment was lost. The methods had been handed down by Eskimos and improved upon.

The first day we constructed an igloo under Dr. Perska's direction. We cut the snow blocks with a large knife. When it was completed Sonja, Dr. Perska, and I crawled inside. The walls I noticed dripped a little.

"Won't the thing melt?" I asked.

Dr. Perska smiled. "Not from simple body heat. The body heat will keep you warm enough to go without a shirt or clothes but it will not melt the blocks of snow. Actually, the melting is good inside the igloo. It seals any drafts caused by gaps between the blocks. Even burning candles in here for light will not come close to melting the blocks."

I looked around at the domed palace. The doctor had already begun to crawl outside again. Sonja reached for my hand, squeezed it.

"Ever make love in an igloo?" she murmured.

"Not for a week or two," I said.

She punched my shoulder and crawled quickly outside. When I followed her and poked my head out the doorway, she blasted me with a snowball.

That night I slept alone, in a chair against the wall, Wilhelmina in my hand. It was not a restful sleep.

The second day we spent mostly in a classroom. Sonja and I sat in comfortable chairs. Dr. Perska stood at a blackboard. We were learning about the

polar bear. The doctor pulled down a screen and
clicked on a projector. For a full minute he just let
the thing run without saying anything. I smoked and
watched.

All the film showed was one polar bear. He was a
big one but to me he looked almost pear-shaped, as
though his back legs were longer than his front ones.
He was never still. He looked clumsy.

"Notice," Dr. Perska said, as if reading my mind,
"how clumsy the bear looks. Many a victim has made
the mistake of thinking that this animal is not capable
of much speed." He was speaking in Russian.

I said, "He looks like he'd have trouble getting out
of his own way."

The doctor was wearing spectacles, the half-round
kind you read through the bottom of and look out at
the world over the top. Now he tucked his chin
against his chest and peered at me over the top of his
specs.

"Mr. Carter, do not make that mistake if you see
one coming from what seems far behind you. You will
be surprised how quickly the gap closes."

Sonja looked at me and winked. We watched the
ambling polar bear again as it galloped slowly this
way and that over the ice.

"The polar bear is a nomad," Doctor Perska said.
"Unlike the grizzly or big brown bear, it does not
have a permanent base or cave. It is always on the
move. The camera has been on our friend here for
quite awhile . . . did you once see him stop? No, he is
constantly moving."

I lit a cigarette and watched the bear gallop
around. Sonja reached for my hand.

"There is one particularly interesting point about the polar bear," the doctor continued, "it is the only animal on the face of the earth which will deliberately track down, kill and eat a human being. This creature does not need an excuse like a cub, to protect, to attack. It does not have to be cornered, like most animals." He looked up at the screen with a wry smile. "No, all this fellow needs is to be a little bit hungry."

I felt Sonja shiver beside me.

"What would it take to bring one down?" I asked Perska.

The doctor scratched his moustache thoughtfully. "I saw one once take four shots from an elephant gun before collapsing. It is possible that only a moose might be harder to kill."

"Or a man," I said, grimly.

That night when most of the compound was asleep, Sonja came to my quarters. I was sitting up in the chair, staring into the fire, thinking about Red Chinese submarines skulking about the Arctic.

The door was locked. Sonja knocked, called "Nick!" softly twice. I got out of the chair and went over to the door, holding Wilhelmina ready . . . just in case.

Sonja came in, ignoring the Luger pointed at her pretty head. She was wearing the same robe she'd had on the other night. It dropped off her shoulders to the floor by the time she reached the bed. The thin gown she wore glowed pink in the firelight.

There was a dreamy smile on her lips. She crawled up on the bed and knelt facing me. Slowly, smiling, she raised her gown up over her head. Then she fluffed out her long blond hair and stretched out on her back. I dropped Wilhelmina in the chair, locked the door and went over to the bed . . .

The third day Sonja and I learned more about how to survive without any equipment. In the building we had labeled the lecture cabin, Dr. Perska stood at the blackboard. Today he wore gray pants and a gray sweater that buttoned down the front.

At breakfast Sonja had held my hand and took every opportunity to touch me, or brush up against me. Last night had been one of the best. Only once, in Corsica, had it been better. I thought maybe I was wrong not to trust her. When she'd held my hand, I noticed she was still wearing the ring the enlisted men on the sub had given her.

Dr. Perska was discussing fishing and hunting— without an expensive rod and reel or rifle. "You can make fishhooks from the bones of a wolf or bear, even from the bones of a fish—" he smiled "—to catch other fish. See the drawings on the blackboard. Line can be made from many things. Thread from your clothing, the sinews of an animal you have killed.

"A bone can even be used to bring down the mighty polar bear. Part of a seal's backbone, for instance. Whale bone is ideal, but it is unlikely that two people alone in the Arctic without equipment would go hunting whale."

He picked up some chalk and sketched as he talked. "You curve the bone, which is normally straight, into a tight circle. Meat or blubber, or whatever you have handy, is packed tightly around it, tight enough to keep the bone from straightening. Shoving the ball of meat around in the snow helps to freeze it, the polar bear will gulp the ball down in one bite. The bone straightens and tears and slices at the bear's insides."

I was impressed, but Sonja shuddered. "The poor creature," she said.

Dr. Perska smiled and shook his head. "My dear Miss Treshenko, you would not think 'poor creature' if you were starving and cold and that poor creature was your only hope of survival."

He put down the chalk, turned—not smiling now— and looked at me.

"Mr. Carter, tomorrow morning you too will fly to the Arctic, then we shall see how well I have taught you, how much you have learned." The smile reappeared. "Are you properly impressed?" he asked.

"Very," I said, and I meant it.

"Good," he nodded. "Now, it is time then to meet your guide."

Guide? I frowned and straightened up in my chair as the doctor went over to the door. He opened it, called to someone. The someone came in, wearing cold-weather gear and carrying an ancient bolt-action rifle. He shoved the hood of his parka back, and I saw that he was an Eskimo—or certainly looked like an Eskimo.

Dr. Perska took him over to the blackboard right in front of us. "Miss Treshenko, Mr. Carter, this is Aku Esau. He has been chosen as your guide for two reasons. One, he is a crack shot and two, he knows the Arctic like ... how is it you Americans say it, Mr. Carter? Ah yes! Like the back of his hand."

I leaned back in my chair and stretched my legs out in front of me, my arms folded. This was something I hadn't expected, something I wasn't prepared for. It wouldn't be just Sonja and me out there in the Arctic. It would be Sonja and me and a guide named Aku.

I stared at him. He looked young, barely over the legal age for drinking and voting. His eyes seemed clear and sure, but they shifted uneasily under my stare. To me he looked like a lad who had a way with the ladies. There was an almost arrogant confidence about him. His face was broad and flat and smooth; his straight black hair hung partly in his eyes. He kept the rifle he held pointed toward the floor. He was standing close enough for me to read the Russian legend on the barrel.

"Mr. Carter?" Dr. Perska said uneasily.

There was tension in the room. Aku kept looking from Sonja to me and back again, but there was nothing in his face that I could read.

"I hadn't counted on a guide," I said finally. I fished out a cigarette and lit it.

"Do you disapprove?" Sonja asked. She went on hastily, "Since we do not know what we are going up against, I for one believe we should take all the help offered."

"I'm sure you do," I said. I looked at her. And just when I was beginning to think I could trust her.

Then, in very good English, Aku said, "Mr. Carter, if you take me with you, you may be pleasantly surprised. I am an excellent guide and an excellent shot—I can shoot the eye out of a seagull at twenty yards. But, more important than that, I know how to follow orders. I know that you will be in charge. I am not asking you to take me, but I think I would be an asset."

I smoked my cigarette and watched his eyes. "Why do you carry a Russian rifle?" I asked.

"I come from a poor family," he said quickly. "We could not afford an expensive American Marlin or Winchester. We could only trade for whatever was available. As a boy, I traded six fox furs for this old rifle. It has saved my life nine times. It puts food in my belly. I treat it and look on it as an old friend. I have never owned any other rifle."

It was a beautiful speech. Beautiful. I looked at Dr. Perska, then at Sonja. I couldn't read anything in their faces. Then I looked back at Aku. "Okay," I decided. "We've got ourselves a guide."

The tension lifted. Aku grinned, showing strong, even, white teeth. Dr. Perska flashed his gold caps. Sonja took my hand and smiled at me. The only one in the room who wasn't smiling was me.

That night I finished packing early. The plane was supposed to take off at dawn. I had transferred everything from the suitcase to the back pack, leaving my suit and overcoat in the suitcase. It wasn't likely I'd go formal in the Arctic.

It was too early for bed—I didn't feel tired. I threw some wood on the fire and sat down in front of it. But I was restless. I stood and prowled the room.

I stopped pacing and stared into the fire. This was my last night at the compound. The only thing I would miss about the place would be that magnificent fireplace.

I checked again to make sure I had packed extra clips for Wilhelmina. Then, sitting in front of the fireplace, I stripped, cleaned and oiled the Luger.

Next, I checked the Winchester I had brought with me.

I was still restless.

I tried Yoga. I sat in the chair staring into the fire and forced my body to relax. I used all my concentration in the effort. I don't know how long I sat that way, relaxed, but when I came out of it I felt refreshed. And I wanted a woman. I wanted Sonja.

I pulled on my parka and heavy boots. Sonja's cabin was across the way and three down from mine. When I was ready, I opened my door enough to peer out. There was light coming from her window. She was still up.

A light snow was falling and my boots crunched as I walked. The bright lights at each corner of the compound gleamed through the falling snow. A guard passed under one of the lights, his rifle on his shoulder.

I walked slowly, my hands deep in the pockets of my parka. Then, as I neared Sonja's cabin, I heard voices. Sonja and . . . I didn't recognize the second voice at first, not until I was almost up to the cabin. I froze. It was Aku, and he was speaking in Russian.

"Moscow is impatient, Sonja," he was saying. "They wish to know when. They wish to know why there has been a delay."

"The decision of when was left up to me," Sonja countered. "It was stupid of them to send that trawler captain."

"They are impatient. Perhaps they acted hastily, but they want it done and they want to know when. They want to know exactly when."

There was silence for a moment. Then Sonja said,

"I have been training for this for two years. I will not
fail. I am not a man. That has been the problem—
sending men to kill him. Every country has made that
mistake. That is why no one has been able to assas-
sinate the great Nick Carter. Only a woman can get
close enough to him to do it. So, where others have
failed, I will succeed. I am already quite close to
him."

"But *when*, Sonja?" Aku asked again.

"As soon as we find out what the Chinese are up to
in the Arctic, as soon as the mission is completed.
That is when I will kill the elusive Mr. Carter,"
answered my beloved Sonja.

SIX

I wasn't close enough to the cabin for them to hear the crunch of my boots in the snow as I backed away. Automatically, I wrapped my right hand around the butt of Wilhelmina, under my left armpit.

I was trapped and knew it. The compound was virtually a prison. Even if I could escape, where would I go? I couldn't swim for it—not in that freezing water. And I wouldn't get far by land either, trying to cross a frozen, barren, hostile country.

No, I was on Soviet soil with no avenue of escape. They had me and I knew it. Tomorrow morning I would board a Soviet plane which would carry me and two Soviet agents—one of whom had been trained just to kill me—into the Arctic wasteland.

I walked quickly back to my own cabin. There was no one I could turn to for help, but I did have one advantage. I knew now what Sonja was up to, and she didn't know I knew.

I had suspected it but, still, I was disappointed. Lovely, sweet passionate Sonja. *Face it, Carter, you've been had. She used her body like a Venus Flytrap to sucker you into trusting her.* All right, now

I knew my mistake. It was highly unlikely I would
make the same mistake again.

I reached my cabin, unlocked the door and went
in. The fire was still burning. I peeled off my parka
and heavy boots and got ready to spend the night in
the chair.

Then it dawned on me that I had no immediate
problem. Sonja had told Aku she wasn't going to
make any attempt to kill me until *after* we had found
out what the Chicoms were up to. I thought about
tomorrow. We would board the Soviet transport at
dawn and fly deep into the Arctic. There we would
get whatever we needed that we didn't already have—
like snow scooters and extra gasoline. We would get it
at an *American* base camp. So the answer was simple. When we reached the base camp, I would simply
turn Sonja and Aku in and continue the mission
alone.

I stayed in front of the fireplace, smoking and
staring into the fire, for a long time. Finally, I got up
and went to bed.

One hour before dawn they rapped on my door.
There wasn't much problem waking me, I wasn't in
that deep a sleep. I jumped gingerly out from under
the quilt and bounced around trying to put my pants
on. The fire was out, and the cabin was as cold as the
ashes of love. It was still dark, so I lit one of the
lamps, then finished dressing.

I saw a light on in Sonja's cabin as I stepped
outside. The sky was turning from black to a kind of
dull gray. The snow had stopped falling but there
were at least ten new inches underfoot. I headed for

the mess hall, my pack on my back and my Winchester in my hand.

I had already started breakfast when Sonja joined me. She looked lovely, as always. Her eyes sparkled with what some people would have mistaken for love. As we ate, she chattered about the survival course, about what we might find in the Arctic, about Aku ... by the way, where was he? He showed up when we were almost finished. He greeted Sonja warmly and was very respectful toward me. I felt like a Mafia victim, getting kissed before the kill. But I went along with the gag. I held Sonja's hand and joked with Aku. I wanted to hang on to the only advantage I had.

When we finished breakfast, we stepped outside where a car was waiting for us. Dr. Perska was there to say goodby. I shook his hand, wondering if he knew about the assassination plan. Then our back packs and rifles were loaded on top of the Moskovitch. Sonja sat in the back seat with me, her hand resting on my knee. She leaned her head against my shoulder, and I could smell her perfume. Her hair tickled my cheek.

Aku sat up front with the driver. The road from the compound to the airstrip, just outside Uelen, was badly chewed up and frozen. We took it at a crawl. Sonja's lips brushed my cheek, found my ear.

"I missed you last night, darling," she whispered. "Did you miss me?"

I put my hand on her leg. "Of course," I said.

She snuggled against me and sighed. "It's going to be awfully cold for a long time. There is no telling what we might have to do to stay warm."

"Will Aku take pictures?"

She chuckled deep in her throat. If only she wasn't so much woman, it wouldn't have been so bad I thought. "Of course not, darling," she said. "Aku knows how it is with us. I have explained it to him. He will not bother us."

"Should be an interesting trip," I said dryly.

The Moskovitch was approaching the airstrip where the big transport waited, its props turning. As the car pulled up alongside the plane, two men jumped down from the open plane door. Without a word, they started pulling our gear off the car and hustled back to the plane with it.

The bleak landscape of frozen whites and grays blushed pink under the rising sun. The air was still and cold. Sonja, Aku, and I ran from the car to the waiting plane. The prop wash threatened to blow us back, but we finally got inside and were pleased to find the plane heated.

Sonja, as always, sat beside me. She snuggled close, her face hidden by the hood of her parka. When we warmed up enough, we pushed back the hoods. Aku sat across from us, gazing out the windows, his face expressionless.

The plane was on skis. The engines revved up quite a bit before the skis broke loose of the ice and the plane moved down the runway. Sonja and I jostled against one another as the plane picked up speed. It rattled like an old pickup truck. We moved from side to side, back and forth. But when the skis lifted off, the rattling suddenly stopped. The big plane climbed smoothly over a countryside almost empty of life.

But there was a house here and there, and sometimes a tree. The plane headed east into the rising
sun. Looking out the window, I saw land's end, and
then we were over water. I could feel Sonja's eyes on
me as I sat looking out the window. I wondered what
was running through her mind. Was she trying to
decide which part of my body would be best to slam
a bullet into? Or maybe she hadn't made up her mind
what weapon to use. If not a gun then . . . what.

Sometime later, there was land below. We were
flying over Alaska and northern Canada. And then
there was nothing below but a white emptiness. Now
and then we passed over a small Eskimo village, but
mostly there was only unbroken whiteness, so bright
in the sun it almost blinded me.

Aku slept, his chin touching the front of his parka.
Sonja hugged my arm. I could feel the slenderness of
her body through the clothes she wore as she pressed
against me.

"Is anything wrong, darling?" she asked suddenly.

I looked down at her, frowning. "What makes you
ask that?"

"You're awfully quiet. You have been all morning."

I shrugged. "A lot on my mind. I'm wondering
what we'll find out there."

She smiled, a knowing smile that told me she didn't
believe me. It could also be interpreted as an under-
standing smile. If her darling had things on his mind
he did not wish to discuss with her, so be it. I wished
we'd hurry up and get to the base camp so that I
could get rid of her. She was getting to me.

"What do you think it is, Nick?" she said suddenly.

"What do I think *what* is?"

"The Chinese. What do you think they are doing out there?"

I shook my head. "They have to be building some kind of polar base. Those subs just couldn't stay under the ice that long without one."

"But what *kind* of base? And where?"

Suddenly, she squeezed my arm. "Never mind. We'll find out, won't we?"

"I wish I could be sure."

She smiled. "I know we will find out, Nick. You are the best AXE has to offer. Failure is not part of your make-up."

I didn't have to answer her. One of the plane's crew came along then with three box lunches and handed them to us silently. I shook Aku awake, passed his lunch to him. He ate it and promptly went back to sleep.

Sometime in the middle of the afternoon, the same crewman came along again. This time he was carrying three parachutes.

We each had one dumped into our laps. As I shrugged into mine, I leaned over and looked out of the window. We were about to pass over the American base camp. I could see the large bungalow-style buildings ahead. The largest had a tall mast with the American flag. The flag hung as still as the air around it. But the sky was clear, and the bright sun made the terrain below look like desert.

The base passed under us, then very quickly was left behind. The crewman pulled open the hatch. An icy blast whistled through the plane. I put on my sunglasses and made sure the hood of my parka was fastened tightly around my head. The crewman was attaching chutes to our gear—the food, explosives and back packs.

The plane circled for another pass over the base. Only the terrain immediately around and inside the installation looked smooth and hard. Everywhere else there were crevices and uneven ground which was why the plane couldn't land. A chopper could have made it, but the distance was too far for a helicopter. Besides, the Russians aren't as keen on using 'copters for everything as we Americans. So we had to jump.

I could see the base layout clearly as we approached it. We were too high to make out anything small but still there didn't seem to be any activity. Nothing stirred on the grounds inside the base. The place was as still as the flag on its mast.

Sonja was standing beside me looking out the open hatch. Aku was behind us. I looked at Sonja, and for an instant our eyes met. But then she glanced behind me, and her eyes widened in concern.

"Aku, what is it?" she asked.

I spun around. Aku's face was shining with sweat, the sweat of fear.

"I—I have never jumped . . . before," he croaked.

I smiled at him. "There's nothing to it, my boy," I said, taking his hand and wrapping it around the handle of his rip cord. "All you do is take one step out, count to ten, and pull."

He blinked at me. Then he frowned, trying to concentrate. "Step out . . . count ten . . . pull." He smiled weakly and nodded.

I slapped him on the back. "Just to show you my heart is in the right place, I'll let you go first."

He started shivering then. "N-no ... I do not wish to jump. I ... I do not want to be first."

I grabbed the front of his parka and slowly brought him around so his back was to the open hatch.

"Nick," Sonja said, "what are you doing?"

I paid no attention to her. "Just remember to pull that handle after you count ten," I told Aku.

I looked over at the Russian crewman. His face showed nothing. We were almost over the base now. The Russian dipped his head in a slight nod.

Aku stuttered, "Whe-when do-do I st-start counting?"

"Now!" I stiffened my arms against his chest, shoved him backward out the hatch.

His arms and legs flailed like he was trying to fly. He went out and down, floating in the air. I watched for the white puff of his chute, but it didn't come. He seemed to be gliding, moving slowly behind us, growing smaller.

"My God!" Sonja whispered hoarsely.

We both stood at the hatch watching. Aku was getting smaller and smaller. Then for an instant he seemed to hang suspended. His arms jerked out and up. Something came peeling out of him like the tail of a kite. A pause and then the chute canopy mushroomed open. I heard Sonja sigh in relief.

"He must be a slow counter," I said.

"Or he had a late start. Nick, I think that was a little drastic. No, it was more than that. It was cruel."

"Was it?" I looked at her. "You ain't seen nothing yet, baby."

Her mouth dropped open slightly, and she looked back at me, puzzled.

"Jump," I said.

She blinked, then turned and stepped out the hatch. Almost immediately her chute opened. I stepped out right behind her.

The air was even colder than I had expected. It stabbed like a thousand needles. I looked down and saw that Aku had already hit the ground, just outside the base. Sonja was going to land about ten feet away from him. My shoulders jerked with the pull as my chute filled with air.

By now the shock of the cold had passed. I held onto the chute straps and looked down. The ground was coming up fast. I relaxed and prepared myself for the shock of landing. Sonja and Aku were on their feet and out of their chutes, watching me. Just before I touched down I had a pleasant thought: I was a sitting duck dangling from that chute. If Sonja had carried her rifle with her when she jumped, she could have picked me off easy.

I struck the ice, heels first, and rolled backwards. Even so I slid along the ground a way. I was helpless. Aku could have come up quickly and shoved a knife between my ribs. I reminded myself then that there wasn't going to be any assassination attempt until after we found out what the Chicoms were up to. Or so Sonja had said.

I shrugged out of the chute harness. Aku and Sonja came over to lend me a hand. We looked up and saw other chutes coming down. Our equipment. The plane had banked, turned. The sound of its engines already seemed to be getting fainter.

My main concern now was the base. We were only about a hundred yards from it, yet no one had come out to meet us. All right, I didn't expect a brass band, but somebody should have been out there. Maybe the whole assignment had been called off. Maybe Hawk hadn't been able to get in touch with me?

The first equipment chute hit the ice. Sonja was standing a little behind me. I stepped to the side where I could keep an eye on her.

"Aku," I said, "check the equipment as it comes down and stack it."

Aku shot a look at Sonja, then at me. "Why should I?" he asked, trying to stare me down.

I matched his stare. "Because I told you to," I said evenly. "The only reason you're here is because you said you could follow orders." I grinned mirthlessly. "Besides, I'm bigger than you. And I'll knock the hell out of you if you don't do what I tell you." Sonja took a step toward me. "And will you knock the hell out of me too?"

"If I have to."

"Nick, why are you so hostile all of a sudden?" She took a step toward me. I backed away one step.

The drone of the plane's engines had faded now. The only sound in the icy stillness was the sound of our movement.

Sonja stood still. "I don't understand you, Nick. There's no reason for your attitude."

I smiled grimly. "I know we're three buddies here to do a job, right, darling?"

She frowned, obviously disturbed. Aku had moved away. Evidentally he'd changed his mind about a showdown with me; he was gathering the equipment as it came down.

"Come on," I grabbed Sonja by the arm. "Let's go see why there's no one here to greet us."

We walked toward the base. As we approached the first building, I knew something was wrong. The door was wide open. I took out Wilhelmina, stepped cautiously up to the door. It had been standing open for some time. Snow was piled hip deep in the doorway. I pushed through the snow drift and went inside, still holding on to Wilhelmina. Sonja came with me. We were in an outer office. Most of the equipment was gone, but there was a desk with two pencils on it. The main office beyond didn't even have that; it was empty.

I took Sonja by the elbow. "Come on," I said a little gruffly.

When we were outside again, Sonja said, "What does this all mean, Nick? There were supposed to be men here. We were supposed to receive transportation."

"Something happened," I said. "The place has been stripped."

I went from bungalow to bungalow. When I reached the garage area, I saw an old jeep half-track with no engine and four battered snow scooters with parts missing. I nosed around while Sonja watched from the doorway.

"Maybe we can do something with the scooters," I said. "Two of them look like they might run. I might be able to make another one that works out of the other two."

"But what happened here, Nick?" Sonja asked.

"I don't know," I admitted. I shoved Wilhelmina into my armpit. "You aren't carrying a gun, are you?"

She held her arms out at her sides; her gold-flecked eyes sparkled. "Care to search me?"

I grinned. "I'll take your word for it." We both moved outside. I looked at the camp area we hadn't covered yet and said, "All right, you take the bungalows on the left, I'll take the ones on the right. Maybe we'll find a clue to what happened here in one of them."

As we were about to separate, she said, "Nick, why did you ask if I was carrying a gun?"

"Just curious."

"You've been behaving curiously ever since we left the compound."

"Oh, you noticed," I interrupted. "Well, we'll talk about it later." I pointed to a bungalow across the way. "I believe that's yours over there."

She walked away from me. I watched until she had gone inside, then went into the nearest bungalow on my side. Mine was empty. When I came out, Sonja was coming out of hers. She shrugged, moved on to the next.

We had reached the last two bungalows. I had just stepped inside the one on my side when I heard Sonja cry out. I stepped back outside, looked across at the other bungalow just as Sonja came stumbling out, one hand pressed tightly to her mouth. She almost fell coming down the steps. When she hit the ice, she sank down on her knees.

I started running. It didn't take me long to reach her. "What did you find, Sonja?"

Her eyes were filled with horror. She just kept saying, "There, there," over and over again.

I left her and got Wilhelmina out again. Slowly I

climbed the steps to the bungalow's open door and peered inside.

The first thing that hit me was the smell ... and then I saw them. Probably every man who had been on the base ... thirty or forty of them. They had been killed, stripped, and stacked inside the bungalow like so many logs.

SEVEN

I didn't linger, looking at the bodies ... they were beyond help. I didn't even have tools to bury them. Somehow I would have to get word to the main base and let them know what had happened here. I stepped back outside and closed the door.

Sonja was still on her knees, making quick gagging sounds. I stepped in front of her and looked down. Her face was sick white.

"Come on," I said, helping her to her feet. "You're supposed to be a hardboiled Soviet agent. Surely you're not going to go to pieces over a few American bodies?"

"Stop it!" she shrieked. "What kind of a man are you? Don't you have any compassion for your fellow countrymen?"

"Right now I just have a big hate for whoever did this."

She wasn't too steady on her pins, wobbling a bit, but the color was returning to her face.

"If we're lucky maybe we can make three working scooters out of that junk in the garage," I said, trying to get her mind off what she had seen. I took her elbow and helped her along.

"What . . . about them?" she asked weakly.

I shrugged. "There's nothing we can do."

A slight breeze was blowing now, kicking up snow like sand on a beach, but the sky was clear, and the sun shone like a new silver dollar.

I looked around for Aku and spotted him heading toward the garage from the other end of the base. All three of us reached the building about the same time.

"You take long time," Aku began, then he noticed Sonja's unnaturally pale face and looked from her to me. "What has happened here?"

Sonja told him about it, in Russian. While she explained, I scrounged around for tools to try and salvage the scooters. Two of the machines looked fairly decent. I cleaned the plugs, filed the points, then started them up. They ran all right. Now I had to make another good running one out of the two pieces of junk left.

I turned to Aku who was just standing around watching me. "Get back to our equipment," I said. "Whoever wiped out this base might still be hanging around, and we're going to need that stuff."

For a split-second he just stared at me blankly, his jaw was set, and I thought he was going to give me an argument again. But after a short glance at Sonja, he turned his back and walked away.

The two snow scooters I had to work with were both partly stripped. I picked the one that was most complete to overhaul. A runner was missing as well as several engine parts. Sonja sat on one of the other scooters, watching me as I worked.

"Something has happened, Nick," she said suddenly. "You have changed since we were at the compound."

"I don't have Soviet trawler captains sneaking into my room and trying to kill me every day."

"But that doesn't explain your hostility toward *me*. What have I done?"

I was squatting beside the scooter I was working on, holding a wrench. I said, "Isn't there anything you'd like to tell me, Sonja? A little confession you'd care to make?"

She looked startled. "Of course not. Why should you think I have anything to confess to you?"

"Why indeed." I went back to work.

It took longer than I thought it would. By the time I was finished, my hands were freezing, even under a thick coat of grease, and I'd scraped a couple of knuckles, but I had another snow scooter running.

Sonja and I took the other two scooters and rode them out to where Aku was pacing back and forth in front of the equipment, his rifle over his shoulder. I sent him back for the scooter I'd patched up.

When we had all three scooters there, we loaded them with the equipment, including two five-gallon cans of gas I'd found in the garage. The wind had picked up, and the bright blue velvet sky had faded to a baby blue.

It was mid afternoon by the time we got the scooters loaded. I changed my mind and decided to ride the patched up scooter mainly because Sonja and Aku wouldn't know how to fix it if anything went wrong. They had both been very quiet while we packed. Now they sat on their scooters and watched me as I lashed down the last of the equipment on mine.

I straightened up and pulled my mittens on. "There's fifty square miles to cover," I said. "Aku, I want you to move in a crisscross pattern, search as much ground as possible while we still have daylight."

Aku nodded then he fired up his scooter and Sonja and I did the same.

"Single file," I shouted over the engine noise. "Aku in the lead, then you, Sonja." I wasn't about to let either of them get behind me. Not with what they had in mind for me.

I gave the ghostly base one last look as the others took off. The wind was kicking up snow thick as fog. In the eerie gloom the base camp looked as still and cold as death itself.

I moved off after the others. My popping scooter sounded pretty sick compared to the other two. The wind was howling now, the snow swirling so thick at times I could barely see Sonja in front of me.

If she and Aku had been ready to kill me, this would have been perfect for them. All Aku would have to do was drift a little to the side, speed up enough so he could stop and wait for me to come along, then put a slug through me. But the time wasn't now, if Sonja meant what she said. I'd live long enough to find out what the Chicoms were up to.

We were heading into a full born storm. The shrieking wind blew stinging snow into my face.

The snow blotted out the sun and I had trouble

determining what direction we were heading. Sonja, on her scooter, was a vague blur ahead of me.

But the storm didn't bother me half as much as what we had found back at the camp. Every man wiped out, the base stripped of everything usable. That meant two things: A sizable force of some kind had attacked the base and that force had to be pretty close by to cart off everything there.

It was possible that Chicoms hiding up there weren't too far away. And whatever it was must be important, because wiping out an American base was bad form—even for the Chinese Reds.

That meant I would have to make a decision before long. As I bounced along behind Aku and Sonja, I debated whether or not to kill them both now and continue on alone. There was one very good argument in favor of the move. It would be tough enough watching what was in front of me without worrying about what might come up behind me.

But there was an equally good argument for waiting—at least for a while. I couldn't ride three scooters and there was no way all the explosives and equipment would fit on one scooter. No, I'd have to wait ... which was okay as long as I got to them before they got to me.

The storm was really wicked now, wind and snow flailing at us. I knew we wouldn't be able to continue on much further. The scooters were starting to sway from side to side, buffeted by the wind. I noticed Sonja and Aku had already reduced their speed, and I was about to increase mine enough to catch up and tell them we should find some place to wait out the storm when I heard the crack of a rifle shot. I couldn't mistake it even with that wind whistling in my face.

I saw Sonja's scooter tip up on its right runner, forcing her to angle left. I looked where she was heading. There was a steep drop about thirty yards away. The rifle slug must have hit the scooter from the way it was weaving. As I watched, it jumped high and threatened to tip over.

"Sonja!" I cried. "Look out!" But my shout was lost in the wind.

She was heading straight for the edge of the drop, bouncing and weaving, completely out of control. I speeded up, though I knew I couldn't possibly reach her in time. Then I saw that if I cut to the left, I might be able to head her off. I turned toward the crevice. If whoever had fired that rifle got the urge to fire again, he would have me right in his sights.

As I raced after Sonja, it occurred to me that the Chicoms may have left a guard or two to watch the base and eliminate anyone who came nosing around. That would explain the rifleman. The only other explanation I could think of at the moment was Aku. He could have speeded up far enough ahead, under cover of the storm, to ambush us. In that case the shot must have been meant for me. In the little talk I'd overheard between him and Sonja, Aku hadn't sounded any too keen on postponing my assassination.

Sonja was getting close to the edge. I had speeded up enough to narrow the gap between us. Her machine wasn't weaving any more, but she seemed to be fighting the throttle. My scooter's runners hissed over the snow as I rushed to intercept her. We were on a collision course now, both heading for the crevice.

I reached it first. I got to within five feet of the
drop, then straightened out, running along the edge
as Sonja headed right for me. Her face, seen through
the swirling snow, was a gray blur framed by the
hood of her parka.

She was going to hit me broadside. I raised my
knees to get my feet on the seat, eased off the throttle
and watched as Sonja's scooter hurtled toward mine.
The instant before impact I jumped.

I leaped for Sonja, grabbed her shoulders, and both
of us went over her scooter and down against the
hard-packed snow. We slid along the ground. I heard
the grinding crunch of twisting, tearing metal. There
was a loud screech as both scooters, mated together,
poised on the edge of the crevice. Sonja and I
slid toward them. I tried to twist around, to get my
feet in front of me and stop our slide. I no longer had
hold of Sonja's shoulders, only the fabric of her parka.

I was the first to hit the scooters. Sonja rolled into
me, and I knew we were going to go over the edge.
The scooters went first, tipping out and then down. I
turned back, clawing at the snow. I heard Sonja cry
out. Then we both went over and down.

A wide, icy-covered ledge about nine feet down
saved us. I landed feet first, striking the ledge with
my heels. I teetered, tried to fall forward, but mo-
mentum carried me back. One of the scooters—mine
it turned out—smashed into the ledge. The other slid
off the ledge into a bottomless ice canyon. My scooter
lay on its side near the lip of the ledge. That was
what saved me. I fell back against it and immediately
pitched forward.

For a long time I lay face down in the snow, trying

to catch my breath. My lungs hurt with the effort. Slowly I bent my legs under me, rose to my knee.

I peered into the wind-whipped blinding snow. The ledge was large, I could see that. How strong it was I didn't know. Right now, though, my concern was for Sonja. She lay still, close to the ice wall. I started to crawl over. When I reached her, she was beginning to stir.

"Are you all right?" I shouted against the howling wind.

She was trying to raise herself now to her hands and knees.

I reached out to help her. "Are you hurt?" I shouted. "Anything broken?"

She shook her head. Then her arms were around my neck and she clung to me. For a second I forgot that she was out to kill me. I knew only that I wanted her. Then I looked down and saw her rifle lying in the snow, and I turned away from her.

I pulled the small tent from the equipment on the overturned scooter. We'd have to stay where we were for the time being. There was no sense worrying about Aku. If he found a place to wait out the storm we would see him again. The Eskimo guide must have been through many storms like this.

Right now we had our own problems. The wind felt strong enough to blow us off the ledge, and it was growing dark fast. When we finally managed to get the tent set up, I pushed Sonja inside and crawled in after her.

The tent was the explorer type. There was ample room inside for two people provided they liked each other.

I noticed Sonja had brought her rifle in with her. I brought my own, plus some rope I had plans for. Once inside the tent, out of the wind, we could at least speak to each other in normal tones.

"I—I'm cold," Sonja said, shivering, her face close to mine.

"The only way we're going to keep warm is to generate some body heat," I said. "But, first things first." I took her rifle and pushed it outside the flap of the tent.

She stared at me. "Why did you do that?"

I kissed the cold tip of her nose. "We have to wait out this storm, and I don't want a slug in my brain if I should happen to fall asleep."

"Nick, what do you mean?" She sounded truly bewildered. She was putting on a great act.

I hadn't really planned on answering the question, but suddenly I decided to get everything out in the open.

I decided something else too. I pushed the hood of her parka back from her head, ran my fingers through her long silky hair, then I started unzipping her parka. I also started talking.

I said, "I'll tell you what I mean. Our last night at the compound, I finished packing early and looked around that cozy cabin and thought it looked empty without my girl. So I went looking for her. I thought I'd bring her back to the cabin. We'd have a drink in front of that grand fireplace and talk, or maybe we'd just say nothing. You know, just sort of stare in the fire."

"Nick, I—"

"Let me finish."

She was wearing a coarse sweater under the parka. I moved my hand down to her waist and under the sweater, caressed the smoothness of her skin. Then slowly I moved my hand up.

"So I went looking for my girl. I dressed in my heavy boots and parka and went outside and down to her cabin. But when I got there I heard her talking to someone. I stood outside the window and listened."

Under my exploring hand, I felt her body stiffen. The gray-blue eyes studied me, the gold flecks sparkling like sequins.

"What do you think you heard, Nick?" she asked in a flat voice.

My hand found the softness of her breasts. Sonja was a member of the delightful no-bra group. I cupped a breast so the nipple barely brushed my palm. Her body was still stiff with tension.

Outside the wind raged against the small tent. It howled and whistled and whipped drifts of snow against the slab side of our little shelter.

"I heard my girl and Aku talking," I said evenly. "My girl was telling him how all the other assassins sent to kill Nick Carter had failed mainly because they were men. The same voice that had told me all those lovely things in Corsica, told Aku how a woman could get close to me . . . close enough to kill. Told him how she had been training for that for two years and how as soon as we found out what the Chinese communists were up to, she would kill me."

For a long time Sonja lay silent, her eyes closed, her arms flat at her sides. Then her lips tightened. "Take your hands off me," she said sharply.

I laughed. "No, ma'am."

"There's no reason for us to pretend to be lovers any longer."

"Then it was all an act."

"You are attractive, it was not a difficult part to play."

"And the ring you wear, the one the submarine crew gave you? The way you ran out crying that night because they got to you? That was an act, too, I take it."

She put her hands on my chest and tried to push me away. "Get your hands off me, Nick."

"Tell me that was an act too. Tell me the tears were phony, and the times on the sub you laughed. Tell me that was phony. Just say none of it meant anything to you."

She struggled against me. "There is no longer any reason for us to make love."

I pulled her close to me. "Oh yes there is. I want to see if that was phony too. I want to know if you faked that. You come very unglued when you make love, Sonja. You get all involved, just as though you're enjoying yourself. I don't think you're that good an actress. I'm going to find out."

"No you're—"

My lips came down on hers. At first she twisted her head trying to break away. Her hands pressed against my chest, pushing. My right hand held her closer while my left undressed her.

She fought. She pushed and pounded and twisted, and I really thought her heart was in it. But I wasn't going to be stopped. In a way my life depended on it. If she really was that good an actress, then I was in big trouble.

But the only one in trouble now was Sonja. She struggled against me. She backed to the rear wall of the tent, but I was so close to her she had to take me with her. Twisting and turning, she fought me right up until the moment I entered her.

At that point she seemed to stop breathing. Her nails dug into the sleeves of my parka.

"I hate you," she hissed through clenched teeth. "I hate you for how you make me feel and for what you make me do."

I was moving with her now. "But you enjoy it don't you?"

She held herself away from me, her elbows stiff, her hands flat against my chest. I leaned against her hands until finally her elbows bent, then pressed my chest against her exposed breasts. My lips brushed her cheek, lightly touched the lobe of her ear.

"Damn you, woman," I whispered harshly. "Tell me you enjoy it!"

"Yes!" she cried suddenly. She wrapped her arms around my neck. "Yes! Yes!"

She began to move against me. It was an involuntary movement, one she couldn't control. Her legs parted to welcome me even more.

My lips were close to her ear. "Sonja," I whispered softly, "you will never convince me you fake this."

"No," she said. "You make this part of it so deliciously good."

Outside the small tent the wind still howled. I didn't hear it. But I heard each soft intake of Sonja's breath, heard every moan. I didn't miss one shuddering sigh.

I raised myself to look at her face. There was just

enough light to see her by. Her face was flushed. She frowned, blinked, her breathing became short and quick. Her eyes closed, then suddenly snapped open as something exploded deep inside her. She started by giving out little sighs. The sighs got louder, became sounds of a kind of agony, of terror, but a delicious terror.

, Like a child grabbing a much-wanted toy I gathered her close to me. I ignored her struggle as she tried to catch her breath. I held her tighter than I should have. I held her tight enough to break her back as my own body responded.

Either she blacked out because I held her too tightly or what had happened inside her was just too much for her to take. She collapsed under me. I relaxed, looked down and saw tiny beads of perspiration along her upper lip. There was no fear of the cold now. We were joined and that kept us warm.

She gave a little groan of protest as I raised myself to a sitting position.

"I'm getting cold," she whimpered. Then her eyes widened in surprise. "What are you doing?"

I had the rope around her ankle and mine before she could move. I tied thick knots, then brought the slack under me.

I smiled at her. "Just in case you get to wandering during the night, love."

She struggled slightly as I pulled her close to me again. "I hate you!" she spit in my ear. "I despise you for what you make me do."

"Maybe," I said. "But I think what you're most unhappy about is that you enjoy it."

"It changes nothing, you know," she snapped. "I am still going to kill you."

I still held her close to me. "You can try, and I'll stop you if I can."

"I hate you!" she screamed.

I pulled her head under my chin. "Try to get some sleep," I said. "I may want you again in the morning."

EIGHT

She liked me even less in the morning, although she seemed to enjoy herself more. I took her with the first light. What upset her was that I woke her up to do it.

, I untied us, dressed and crawled outside the tent. It was unbelievably cold, so cold even the clear blue sky seemed to be tinted with ice crystals.

, Standing on the ledge, I felt as if I were on some strange planet. Across from me was the opposite wall of the crevice. It looked like a giant ice cube cut in half. There was whiteness everywhere, so bright I seemed to be surrounded by mirrors. I put my sunglasses on as Sonja came crawling out of the tent.

I grinned at her. "You don't look so bad in the morning. In fact, with your hair all mussed like that and bunched up in your eyes you look damned sexy. If you weren't trying to do me in, I think I'd trot you right back inside that tent."

I held out my hand to her to help her up. She took it, but once she was standing she shoved it away from her.

"You take a great deal for granted," she said.

I stopped smiling. "So do you, Miss Treshenko.

Don't think killing me is going to be easy. It will be the hardest thing you ever had to do ... if you live through it."

We were standing there glaring at each other when a heavy line slapped down into the tent. I looked up and saw Aku peering over the edge of the crevice.

"You're not hurt?" he asked anxiously.

"We are fine, Aku," Sonja answered. They both spoke Russian.

I looked down over the edge of the ledge. It looked like about a two hundred foot drop to where water bubbled. There were other ledges on the way down but none as wide as the one we had landed on. Sonja's scooter had broken apart. We could see pieces of it scattered on some of the ledges.

Seeing what was left of Sonja's scooter reminded me that we had a couple of problems. Some of the extra fuel was on my scooter but most of it had been on Sonja's. More important, her scooter had been carrying all of the food. It wouldn't do any of us a damned bit of good right now to get hungry.

Sonja stooped, reaching for her rifle. I put my foot on the barrel and grabbed it out of her hand. I ejected the clip to her rifle and dropped it into my parka. Then I handed the rifle back to her. She glared at me but she didn't argue.

. Aku was waiting. I tied the rope around my scooter, and with Aku pulling with his own scooter, we managed to get the thing up. We took the tent and the rest of the equipment and piled them together separately. When the scooter was up, we tied the equipment to the rope and Aku pulled that up.

Then it was time for human cargo. I knew I had to

play it cagey or I could easily put myself in a very thin ice situation. Regardless of Sonja's other talents, I didn't trust her any farther than I could personally shot-put a Boeing 747. I trusted Aku equally.

When the equipment was up and the rope came down again, Sonja stepped toward it.

I moved in front of her. "As much as I'd like to be a gentleman, I think I'll go first, Sonja. You understand, don't you, sweetheart? I wouldn't want you both up there with the rope while I waited down here with nothing."

She stepped back. "Help yourself," she said.

I did. I climbed with my rifle over my shoulder on its sling. It was positioned in such a way that I could use it if Aku decided to get cute. He played it straight, and when I was over the lip of the crevice I grinned at him.

"I will put your rifle on the sled," he said innocently.

Still smiling, I handed him the rifle. I watched him closely as he went over to the scooter. Then I heard Sonja coming up the rope. I turned my back on Aku and reached down to help her.

I wanted to find out if Aku was intended to be a back-up assassin.

I got my arms around Sonja and pulled her over the lip of the crevice. No shot came. When Sonja was on her feet, I turned to face Aku. He had a sheepish look on his face.

I went to Aku's scooter and picked up his rifle. He watched me eject the clip and put it in the pocket of my parka.

"This is not wise," he said.

"We'll see."

He shook his head. "Suppose we come up against something and need all of our rifles?"

I shoved the rifle back on the scooter. "I'm going to have enough trouble watching what's in front of me without worrying about a shot in the back."

I started removing some of the equipment from Aku's scooter. I dumped part of the clothing and a small portion of the explosives on the ice beside the scooter. Then I turned back to Aku.

"Who fired that shot at Sonja?" I asked.

. Aku shot a glance at her. To me he said, "It was a Chinese soldier. The wind was blowing but I saw enough to know. I caught a glimpse of a sled and dogs." He gave me a puzzled look. "What is wrong?"

I walked over to my own scooter. "I know you and Sonja are Russian agents. I know Sonja plans to kill me as soon as we find what we came here for."

He didn't seem surprised. For a second he and Sonja looked at each other. She nodded slightly. Aku shrugged and flashed me a quick smile. He rubbed his nose and leaned against his scooter.

"So, what now?" he asked.

I carried the stuff I'd been hauling on my scooter over to his. As I packed it I said, "So now Nick Carter is very careful. I have the clips to both your rifles. Maybe if I keep you both in front of me I'll live a little longer." I had the equipment loaded now and lashed down. I looked over a bleak, cold land. There .was a light breeze, and though the sun was shining it brought no warmth.

"Why have you loaded everything onto my scooter?" Aku asked.

I explained. "The way I figure it the Chicoms aren't
very far from here. Since you're along as guide, I'll let
you continue to guide until we find some kind of
village or settlement. Then I'm going on alone. In the
meantime, you'll take your scooter and lead the way.
Sonja is doubling up with me."

I had to clean the plugs on my scooter before we
could head out. I told Aku to head toward where he
had seen the Chicom. My scooter ran poorly, but it
ran. I kept Sonja sitting in front of me and I stayed
right on Aku's tail.

We stopped once and pulled out a little survival kit
from the stuff on Aku's scooter. In it was fish line and
bait and an auger to bore a hole in the ice. We were
all hungry, and it didn't take us long to clean and get
frying two medium-sized fish we caught.

When everything was cleaned up, I divided the
last of the gasoline between the scooters. We could go
about a hundred and fifty more miles I figured, then
we'd have to abandon them. We started off again.

I didn't trust Aku. How did I know he was really
heading toward where he'd seen the Chicom? He
could be just riding in circles, trying to buy time. On
foot he and Sonja would have the advantage, especially if he went longer than a day or two. I'd have to
sleep; they could take turns.

The bleak terrain looked worse than any desert I
had ever seen, and the wind blew constantly. Our
little scooter engines kept popping and the only other
sound was the hiss of our runners gliding over the
snow.

Then we entered what could be described as a
foothill area. Beyond it, mountains seemed to tower. I

didn't know whether they were really mountains or only high peaks of accumulated ice and snow. But they were directly in front of us. Everywhere else there was the flat, empty, wind-whipped ice.

We headed up a small rise. It wasn't steep but my scooter was just about played out. I had to stop every two hours to clean the fouled plugs. I was right behind Aku. He went up and over the edge of the rise just as I started up. My scooter's engine labored up and, just as I topped the rise and went about a foot along the flat top, the plugs fouled again.

It was as if someone had turned off the key. The thing simply quit running. Aku turned his scooter around and stopped. He turned off his engine, pulled off his mittens and lit a cigarette. Sonja climbed off and stood off to the side. She had been silent most of the day.

This hill was almost like a staircase. What we were on was the first step. There were three altogether, about twenty yards wide and just as long. Sonja and Aku waited while I dug out the tool kit and pulled and cleaned the plugs. I was kneeling in the snow. There was a slight breeze. When the plugs were cleaned and replaced, I pried the lid off the hand cleaner and washed my hands. It was while I was wiping them dry that I saw the smoke.

All day the sky had been a clear velvet blue with the sun a round, frozen ice cube. Now there were wispy curls of dark smoke high above.

I pulled out my binoculars. The source of the smoke seemed to be somewhere over the top of the hill.

"Wait here," I told Aku and Sonja.

I climbed up the second step of the hill, then the third. From there I could see that the smoke was a single column. It was solid close to the ground, but as it rose it fanned out. The mountains were to my right, the bleak flat waste to my left. I looked at the smoke column through my binoculars.

It was a village, I saw, a settlement, about twenty miles away. From what I could see, it wasn't very big. The smoke seemed to be coming from a shack, the kind Eskimos use for smoking fish or meat. There were one or two small buildings, but it was too far away to make out any igloos.

I wondered if Aku had been leading us there all along. We had been heading in that general direction. I didn't know. Maybe I would be walking into a trap. On the other hand, maybe Aku didn't know about the village. Then I could do something about him and Sonja. And there was the possibility that someone in that settlement had seen or heard something unusual in the area. The Chicoms were close, I was willing to bet on it.

The wind tore at my parka, and I braced my legs as I studied the land around. I made a 360-degree sweep with the binoculars over the flats we had just left. I could make out our scooter tracks extending like railroad tracks as far as I could see. Then I saw something else.

Because they were the same color as the snow, I almost missed them. There were three polar bears coming along the tracks. Two were adults and the third was a cub. They did not move either to the left or right of the scooter tracks but straight along them. They looked clumsy and slow like the bear in the film

Dr. Perska had shown, and seemed to be moving at a sloppy trot. That was when I made my first mistake. They were a couple of miles away and I didn't think we'd have to worry too much about them.

Aku watched me closely as I came back down the hill. He kept studying me as I repacked the binoculars.

I turned toward him, lighting a cigarette. "Did you know the settlement was there?" I asked.

"Yes," he said. "I knew."

"Were you taking us there?"

He didn't answer. Sonja watched us both, looking first at him, then back at me.

"It doesn't matter," I said. "We're heading there anyway. I'm going to leave the two of you there and go on alone." I jerked my thumb over my right shoulder. "By the way a couple of polar bears with a cub are tracking us."

Aku stiffened. "How far back?"

"A couple of miles. I figure we can outrun them on the scooters. If not, I'll put them away."

He took a step toward me. "You *must* give me the clip to my rifle, you *must*."

"No way," I said evenly. "Now crank up that stallion of yours and let's get this show moving."

We drove at about ten to fifteen miles an hour. Sonja sat stiffly in front of me, trying to avoid any body contact. But now and then we hit a bump and she would be pushed back against me.

About an hour's riding and my plugs fouled again. We went through the same scene: Aku sat and smoked, Sonja stood and watched, and I dug out the tool kit.

. I worked quickly, automatically. Finished, I cleaned my hands and put the tools away. Then I stood and looked ahead, toward the horizon. I could make out the buildings of the settlement with the naked eye now. Then I looked back in the direction we had come from.

I was shocked at the speed those polar bears were moving! They were less than half a mile away and closing fast. They still looked ridiculous, lumbering clumsily along.

. Aku, beside me, had seen them too. He screeched and pawed at the pocket of my parka.

I slapped his hands away. "Get back to your scooter!" I ordered. "I'll take care of them."

"No!" His eyes were wild. "I must have my rifle clip. I must be able to use my rifle. Please! You must give me that clip!"

I stared at him. Even Sonja, I saw, seemed puzzled at his behavior. I said again, "Get back to your scooter. I'll take care of them."

I pushed him away and slid the Winchester out of the pack on the back of my scooter. Aku screeched and backed away from the scooters. I ignored him. The bears were moving at incredible speed. They were less than a hundred yards away now.

I moved five steps behind the scooters, carefully peeled the scope cover off the rifle, then wrapped the sling around my left wrist. I stood waiting, my legs slightly apart.

The bears were close enough now for me to see their lolling tongues. They ambled in an almost zig-zag pattern with the cub between them. I noticed that their fur was not the stark white it had looked at a distance, but a dirty cream color. They did not look menacing or mean, only a little stupid. But they kept zigzagging toward us. Now they were less than fifty yards away.

I brought the butt of the Winchester to my shoulder. I knew the big-bore rifle was going to give one hell of a kick when I fired it—the thing was designed to bring down elephants. I rested my cheek against the smooth stock. The bears were 25 yards away . . . twenty.

Keeping both eyes open, I looked through the scope. I decided to take out the cub first. That might confuse the others long enough for me to get a bead on one of them.

I had the cub's chest centered in the crosshairs of the scope. I sucked in my breath and held it. I could hear the bears panting now. In the scope they looked to be right on top of me.

. Then I heard Aku. He began to run, screeching hysterically, off to my right. But the bears were too close now for me to think about anything else. They were ten yards off and bearing down on me.

Slowly I began squeezing the trigger. I braced myself for the kick when the rifle fired, then I squeezed the trigger all the way.

There was no kick because the rifle didn't fire. All I heard besides the panting bears was a sickening click.

The firing pin slammed into an empty cartridge.

NINE

The bears were snarling. I ejected the dud cartridge, slowly squeezed the trigger again. The same empty click. And then I knew there was no point in trying again.

Stumbling backward, I started to run as fast as I could. Sonja and Aku were already running. But the bears were too close. We'd never outdistance them. In desperation, I dropped the Winchester and fished under my parka for Wilhelmina. There was no time to aim perfectly. Besides, with the killing power of the Luger I figured I could hit the cub just about anywhere and it would be dead. I squeezed off two shots. They echoed off the sides of the mountains with such volume I felt sure they must have been heard in the settlement.

Without a sound the cub pitched forward and somersaulted tail over head. It slid under the feet of the bear on its left. Both bears broke their stride to look down at the cub. One stopped and circled the bleeding cub quickly. The other kept on coming but slower.

I fired at him. The slug slammed into its neck. It dipped its head, skipped a step, but kept right on coming. I fired again, saw a chunk of the big head chip away. But the bear only shook its head as though shooing away a fly. I was stumbling backward now, watching the creature, fascinated as I fired the Luger again and again. Each time a slug slammed into the bear's chest it hesitated, then gathered itself and kept coming.

Blood was pouring from the bear's head and chest. It reared up on its back legs, came down on all fours again. The front legs buckled and it went down, its head sliding on the ice. I kept moving back, my left hand holding my gun wrist to keep it steady. I raised the Luger as the bear once again raised itself on all four legs.

It staggered toward me. The snarls coming from its throat were unlike anything I had ever heard. It came at me like a drunk, stumbling, staggering, head dipping then rising. I fired again and it paused. Then I fired the last shell in Wilhelmina.

The bear's front legs buckled again. The huge head bobbed and dipped toward the ice. He was close enough for me to feel the heat of his breath. The eyes closed, opened, then closed again. The snarls weakened, became gurgles as the huge body swayed back and forth, then finally toppled to one side. The creature lay still except for one quivering hind leg.

I heard Aku scream. Quickly, I scanned the area. Sonja was far enough away to be out of danger. But the second bear had started after Aku. It lumbered along quickly closing the distance. Aku turned and started to run.

I ran back to the scooters, digging into the pocket of my parka for the clip to Sonja's rifle. I yanked the rifle off the back of the scooter, slammed the clip home . . . just as the bear caught up with Aku.

The bear was all over him, pawing and snapping his teeth. Aku had his knife out, stabbed wildly at the thing.

I ran toward them. Out of the corner of my eye I saw Sonja watching in fascinated horror. The bear looked as if it were boxing with Aku. It swiped at him, kept bobbing its head in and out. Aku had stopped screeching. He seemed to go limp as the bear snapped at him, twisting its giant head.

. Sonja's rifle was against my shoulder. I fired and the butt jerked against my shoulder. The bear's head bounced to the side, then snapped back. It turned toward me and I saw a gaping hole where its left eye had been. Aku was forgotten now; he lay still at the bear's feet.

The huge creature started for me. It took one step and I fired again. The second shot took its nose away. I cocked and fired quickly a third time through what I hoped was a lung. The bear let out a yelp, turned completely around and sat down. Then it rose and started for me again.

I hit it with a fourth shot. It stiffened and stood perfectly still with its head down, looking like a bull ready to charge. It swayed from side to side on weakening legs. I pulled the bolt of the rifle back, heard the click as the shell ejected. I could feel the heat of the barrel. I shoved the bolt forward and, almost without aiming, I fired again.

The bear started to take one more step. The paw lifted, was extended forward like the paw of a big shaggy dog wanting to shake hands. And then the bear simply fell to the side like a chopped redwood. Its huge body split the frozen surface snow when it hit.

I stood looking at the creature along the barrel of the rifle. Then, slowly, I put the weapon down. My heart was pumping so hard I felt a pain in my chest. The silence was so total now it seemed to plug my ears. I noticed the ice and snow around me was spattered with blood. I looked up and saw swirls of smoke passing overhead, drifting with the wind.

. I heard someone running. Sonja dodged in front of the scooters toward Aku. I didn't think he could be alive, he seemed to be covered with blood.

I felt strange. Within me was an unbelievable feeling of calm. Before there had been no time to think. Everything I had done I had done strictly by instinct. But now that it was over, I had time to reflect.

They were magnificent creatures, these polar bears. I had killed three of them and it was unlike anything I had experienced before. I looked from one huge carcass to the other, and I knew the heart of a hunter. This was something to tell your grandchildren about. I knew that years from now, when I thought about it, I would still feel the same excitement.

I dropped the rifle and walked slowly over to where Sonja knelt beside Aku. "How bad is he?" I asked.

Sonja had peeled back the guide's heavy parka. "He is very bad, Nick," she said, without looking up at me. "As you can see, his face is torn open and he has bad bites all over his left shoulder. I think his right leg is broken too."

"But he's alive."

"Yes," she said, "he is alive."

Aku begin to stir. His eyes opened and immediately went wide with fear. "N-no!"

"It's all right," Sonja said soothingly. "The bears are dead. Nick killed them and saved your life."

Aku looked up at me. His eyes seemed to have trouble focusing.

"Why?" he asked, weakly. "You know we mean to kill you. Why?"

. Sonja looked at me then. "Yes, Nick, why? Yesterday when I was heading for that crevice, you blocked the way."

I grinned at her. "Maybe I like a challenge," I said. "Come on. We'd better get Aku some help. Let's get to that settlement!"

"I did it," Aku mumbled then. I had to listen hard because he was running his words together. "It is my fault your rifle did not fire. When we reached that American base camp I did not stay with the equipment. I, too, searched. I found a clip that would fit your rifle. I broke the cartridges apart and emptied them of gunpowder, then I hid the clip in my parka. I waited for a chance to switch it for your full one. It came at the crevice while you were helping Sonja up the rope. You handed me your rifle . . . remember?" Saliva was trickling out of the corners of his mouth.

I remembered and I understood why he was so anxious to get his own rifle clip back. He knew I wouldn't be able to stop those bears.

Sonja fetched the First-Aid kit. While she patched up Aku as best she could, I rearranged the equipment on the scooters. I had them repacked again when

Sonja came up to me. There was blood on the sleeves of her parka and the knees of her pants.

She was sniffling with the cold and rubbed her nose with the back of her mitten. "You didn't really answer my question," she said. "You only avoided it. Why did you save my life when you knew what I was? And just now, why did you save Aku?"

I couldn't answer her. I couldn't tell her why because I didn't know why myself. It was just that no matter what she was, I couldn't have let her go careering over the edge of that crevice without trying to save her, any more than I could stand by and watch a bear chew up Aku.

I said as much. She stood there listening, looking at me, her face expressionless. If she didn't understand me, I certainly didn't understand her. There had been her passion on Corsica, and there had been her tears aboard that sub. I looked at the classic beauty of her face, framed by the parka, at the tip of her nose and her cheeks rosy with cold. I still felt something, some kind of bond between us, and I couldn't believe it was all one-sided. Surely she must feel it too.

I sighed. "We'll load Aku on my scooter. You'll sit on it and steer while I tow you both. I think that's the best way."

"Whatever you say, Nick." She turned her back on me and walked back to Aku. I watched her go.

Okay, I told myself, you're not some starry-eyed teen-ager with his heart in his hand. She's a Soviet agent with a mission. Her orders were to get close to me—and she had—and kill me. Well, if she tried, I would kill her first.

We got Aku loaded on my scooter. Then, with

Sonja steering it, I towed them toward the settlement.

The going was agonizingly slow. The scooters barely had enough power to tow all that equipment plus
three people.

I figured when we got to the village I'd tell the
people about the dead bears. From what I understood about the Eskimos, giving those bears to them
would buy us just about anything we needed.

We had been traveling about an hour when I saw
something heading from the settlement toward us. I
halted the scooter, and went back to where Aku was
strapped to the second scooter. I reached in his pocket and pulled out the good clip to my rifle. The
Winchester loaded and the clips to the other two
rifles in my pockets again, I waited, leaning against
my scooter, for whoever was coming.

There were three dog sleds. Each had an Eskimo
woman in the seat and a man driving. One sled
pulled up on our left, another on our right. The third
stayed directly in front of us.

The driver on my left had a rifle in the crook of his
arm. His broad, flat face stretched in a weak smile.
Then he got off the sled and walked toward me. The
dogs were barking and snarling at each other. The
women looked curiously at Sonja.

The man coming up to me wore a furry parka. His
rifle, I saw, was an old military Enfield 303. His dark
face was blank as he took in both scooters and the
equipment, before his almond-shaped eyes fixed
themselves on my face.

"American?" he asked. He had a deep voice.

I nodded. "We have an injured man."

He grunted and let that pass. "We hear shooting."

I nodded again. "We left three polar bears back there. Dead. You are welcome to them. All we want is help for the injured man."

He gave me a big smile now, showing horse teeth. He had the kind of face that never aged. He could have been anywhere from 26 to 66. He rattled something off to the others in a language I'd never heard before.

The three women jumped from the sleds. They waddled on heavy legs over to where Aku was strapped on the second scooter and started making female noises as they fussed over him.

With the Eskimo's help, we got Aku loaded onto one of the sleds. The driver turned it around and started back toward the village. Sonja and one of the women went with it.

The man with the horse teeth pointed behind me. "You lead us to bears?"

"Yes," I said. The men looked startled when I started the scooter. But the noise of the engine was soon drowned out by the loud barking of the dogs. About to move out, I looked off toward the mountains . . . and froze.

On the crest of a hill I saw a man silhouetted against the sky. There were also dogs and a sled. The man was watching us through binoculars.

I realized then that more than bears had been following our trail.

TEN

It was dark by the time we got the bear carcasses back to the settlement. I had learned that the head of this particular clan was a man named Lok. The other members of the clan were Lok's sons and their wives and *their* sons and their wives. The settlement was just a temporary place for them, during the winter.

There were eight igloos besides the smoke house. One of the igloos was larger than the average family place. This was a sort of community center where children played, and the men and women exchanged gossip. This was where I met Lok.

He looked about a hundred and fifty years old. He spoke no English but his son, the one who had led the group that came out to meet us, served as interpreter.

The igloo was both warm and humid. Candles burned giving off the only light. Old women sat around the walls chewing on skins to soften them.

I was offered whale blubber and raw fish which I ate hungrily. The Eskimos watched me with a mild, amused curiosity.

The community igloo stank of stale body odors, burning candle wax and bear grease. The candles gave out a weaving, glimmering light. As I ate, sitting

111

cross-legged on a hide next to Lok, I watched the women working. The oldest of them had their teeth worn almost to the gums from chewing hides.

I learned two things while I ate. Aku had gotten the best attention these people could give. His leg had been set, the bites dressed, the face stitched. It would take time, of course, for his wounds to heal, but Aku was going to be all right. I also learned that Sonja had been so exhausted she had gone to sleep in one of the other igloos.

The son of Lok was named Drok. He sat across from me, watching me closely. He was as inquisitive as a child, but there was nothing else childish about him, and he seemed proud that he could speak English.

"I have been Anchorage," he said, sticking out his chest. "I only one in family who go to Anchorage."

I stuffed some more raw fish into my mouth. "How long were you there?" I asked.

He held up dirty fingers. "Six months. Long enough to learn American, huh?"

I grinned and nodded. "You learned it well."

He grinned back, showing those horse teeth. He looked around the igloo. Without pausing in their chewing, all the women grinned and nodded.

Then Lok spoke up. Drok listened attentively, still grinning. When his father finished speaking, Drok again swept a look around the igloo. He focused, finally, on a young girl who sat at the end of the group of chewing women. She was chattering to two other women sitting on each side of her. She was a lovely thing, about 16 I guessed, with smooth skin and a bright smile. She saw Drok looking at her and bowed her head in shyness.

Drok turned back to me. "My father have three daughters. No one chosen yet." He pointed to the young girl. "She youngest." He slapped my arm again. "They like you. They will laugh with you. You choose any you want, but young one best."

I looked over at the girl. Her head was still bowed shyly, but she sneaked a look at me. Then she put her index finger to her lips and giggled. The women on each side of her giggled too. So did everyone else in the igloo.

I didn't want to offend anyone, especially after the hospitality the Eskimos had shown. They had taken us in, tended to Aku's wounds, fed me and now they offered me one of their girls.

I said, "I thank you for the honor, Drok. Please thank your father for me. But I must refuse. There is someone I am already laughing with."

He raised eyebrows. "Skinny one who with you?"

I nodded, watched and waited while Drok relayed the answer to Lok. The old man listened in silence, watching me. Then he frowned and grunted something to Drok.

Drok grinned at me again. "My father not understand you choose one so pale and skinny. There no meat on her." He nodded to the young girl. "That one plenty meat. She keep you warm on cold night. She give you many, many babies. She young, have many years left."

"I thank you again for the offer, but I have already chosen."

He shrugged.

Drok had his Enfield rifle beside him, and his hand

always rested on it. Now I asked, "Drok, how many others in the settlement have rifles?"

"None," he said proudly. "I have only one. I great shot. I best shot in all Frozen Land."

"I'll bet you are." I didn't have to ask any more. The only way anyone would get that rifle from him would be over his dead body.

Lok said something more to Drok. There was a long pause before Drok relayed the message to me.

"My father told me he worry. You give us two bear hides, and meat of bear cub is good, and you not take daughter. He not know how he pay you for such gifts."

I leaned back, took out a pack of my cigarettes and offered them to father and son. Each took one and lit it with relish. Drok coughed with the first puff but kept at it.

I said, "Tell Lok there is a way he can repay me, if that is his wish. I would like to know if he, or you, or anyone here in your settlement has seen anyone else besides us in the last week or month ... any strangers."

Drok translated this for his father. There was a long silence. The old man was frowning. Drok waited respectfully. Finally, the old man shook his head and grunted something.

"He has seen nothing," Drok said, "but he very old. He not see well any more. *I* see strangers."

I leaned forward. "You have?"

Drok let his eyelids droop. He held the half-smoked cigarette out and looked at it down his nose. He knew both his father and I were watching him closely. He was the center of attention and he was enjoying the position.

"Yes," he said finally. "I see men. Always with sleds and dogs. Always far away."

"What were they doing, these men?"

He pursed his lips and continued to study the smoking cigarette. "Nothing."

"They must have been doing *something*," I protested. "What was it?"

Drok put the cigarette to his lips and sucked in some smoke. He blew it out without inhaling. "They stand on mountains, I think. And they look at igloo through glasses."

"They were watching this settlement then."

"Yes. I think."

"How were they dressed? Did they have on any kind of uniforms?"

Again Drok waited a long time before answering, sticking his lower lip out, his eyelids still half closed. "I think no," he said at last. He shrugged. "They stand on crest looking through glasses. They too far away see how they dressed."

I mashed out my cigarette. "Drok, would you ask your father if it would be all right for me to take one of the polar bear hides? I want to borrow it for awhile. I'd bring it back."

Drok relayed this to his father. Lok nodded and rattled something off to one of the women. A bear hide was brought to me and dropped at my feet.

Drok said, "Where you go?"

"I'll be leaving the village for awhile. But there is something I must do first." I pushed myself to my feet with the hide in my arms. "Thank you for your hospitality, Drok. Will you please thank your father for me?"

I left the igloo and crossed over to where the scooters and equipment had been left. Both Sonja's and Aku's rifles were there. It took me half an hour to pull all the clips in the packs, plus the ones in my pack, and empty all the cartridges of gunpowder. That done, I palmed the clips I had been carrying into the rifles. Now there were only two rifles that would fire. My Winchester and Aku's ancient Enfield.

I pulled Wilhelmina out of her holster, ejected the Luger's empty clip and replaced it with a full one. From one of the packs, I pulled an extra clip for the Winchester and stuffed it in my pocket. Next I emptied one of the back packs and refilled it with explosives and detonators. I put an extra parka and the first-aid kit on top. Then I slipped the back pack on and adjusted the straps until they felt comfortable.

I picked up my Winchester and headed away from the settlement, hung the binoculars over my left shoulder. I had a definite destination in mind. I was heading for the hill where I had seen the man with the sled.

I moved in a half trot. I figured it would take me the better part of an hour to get there. Every ten minutes I stopped, raised the binoculars to look all around. If the man was still around, I didn't want to fall into a trap.

Whatever the Chinese were hiding, it was nearby— I could feel it. Why else would anyone be watching the settlement? Why else would anyone follow the scooters? Why else wipe out an American base?

The polar bear hide was wrapped around my

waist. That plus the weight of the pack forced me to rest often. It took longer to reach the first of the hills than I had figured. In fact, it took almost three hours.

I went up the hill slowly. Beyond it were two others, which stretched in the mountains. It was not a steep climb but it was tiring because of all the weight I was carrying. When I finally reached the crest of the hill I wanted, I was breathing hard. I sat down and rested my head in my hands.

A light breeze was blowing, as cold as the breath of death, when I got to my feet and began searching the area. There hadn't been enough wind to cover all signs. The man and his dog sled must have left tracks. The tracks would show me where they had gone when they left the hill.

I moved in half-circles, studying the ground. Actually, it wasn't tracks I saw first, it was dog dung. Then I saw the sled tracks. I figured the direction, started off again in a half trot.

I kept moving between the runner tracks. They led down the opposite side of the next hill, around another toward the mountains. The tracks took the easy way into the mountains, through a narrow canyon, around the base of a narrow mountain. And then I was entering a long valley surrounded by mountain peaks that reached so high their tips were lost from view.

It was a Christmas card world. Here and there were ice coated pines. A creek gurgled down through the middle of the valley. Evidently the high mountains kept the killing Arctic winds from ripping through the spot. The air here felt at least thirty degrees warmer.

The sled tracks led through the valley, the tracks suddenly ended. I had moved past them and doubled back to make sure. I knelt, frowning.

The tracks had stopped, disappeared. It was as if something had plucked sled, dogs, and man off the face of the earth.

Ice Bomb Zero was warming up.

ELEVEN

Puzzled, I stood and looked all around me. The mountains were tall but they were not thick. Beyond them stretched the Arctic Sea with its permanently frozen ice cap, the largest glacier on earth, constantly moving and melting. But this valley was land. It was frozen to be sure but it was still land, not ice.

Something had made that sled disappear. I pulled a pencil flashlight out of my pocket and knelt where the tracks ended. I studied them closely. It was as if they had been cut, literally.

"What the hell?" I said aloud.

I didn't know "what," but was going to find out. I unwrapped the polar hide around my waist, let it drop to the snow. I figured I would have to wait if I was going to find out anything. The sled disappeared suddenly, it would reappear just as suddenly. I would be there when that miracle happened.

Swishing the bear hide back and forth to erase my tracks I moved away from where the sled marks ended. I kept going for some distance, then I stopped. I pulled the rifle and binoculars off my shoulder and, leaving the pack on my back, stretched out on my stomach and pulled the bear hide over me.

I waited, keeping the binoculars trained on the spot where the sled tracks ended. An hour passed. It was uncomfortably hot under that bear skin. I knew now why polar bears could swim the icy waters of the Arctic. Another hour passed. I was almost smothering. And then finally something happened.

Even though I watched the miracle through binoculars, I still couldn't quite believe what I saw. The spot where the sled tracks ended was the edge of a trap door. But this was no ordinary run-of-the-mill trap door. Part of the earth tilted up revealing a gaping cavity. I watched with my mouth open. The huge door kept going up and up, creaking, scraping, lifting frozen snow and ice with it, a gaping mouth twelve feet high and at least twice as wide. Noise belched out of the dark opening, sounds of hammering, pounding ... of things being built. I saw a large icy ramp leading down from the opening. It wasn't steep, perhaps a 30-degree angle, but it led into darkness and I couldn't see anything more.

Warm air filtered out of the opening, enough for me to feel it on my partly covered face. It began to melt the snow around the hole, but when the huge door closed again that snow would quickly refreeze, helping to seal the edge of the door.

Then, above the din of activity from below, I heard a sharp scraping sound. I snuggled back into the protection of the bear skin, keeping the binoculars glued to my eyes, and my eyes glued to the trapdoor opening.

The scraping sound was the noise of a sled pulled by nine dogs. It came up the ramp into view and in a minute was gliding away on the snow. With more scraping and screeching, the huge door began to close. There was a loud whoosh as the door shut, sealing off all gaps. I shifted my binoculars from the door to the sled.

There was one man with the sled. He was heading toward the canyon between the high mountain peaks, about two hundred yards away. He reached it and halted the dogs. I saw him pull out binoculars and start to climb one of the short peaks.

I was on my feet, the bear skin still over me. I started running in a crouch, heading for the sled driver. I had got a good look at him, good enough to know he was Chinese and good enough to recognize the brown uniform of the People's Army. There was no doubt in my mind now. I had found the Chicom base. Now all I had to do was get in there.

I approached the dogs cautiously. Two of them were snarling at each other. The rest watched without any apparent interest. The Chinese soldier was on the rise, gazing through his binoculars at the Eskimo settlement far below.

I circled around the dogs and started up the side of the hill. About halfway up I dropped the bear skin and eased the pack off my shoulders. I gently placed the Winchester in the snow. A shrug of my shoulder, and Hugo, my stiletto, dropped into my hand. On hands and knees, I crawled the rest of the way.

As I eased over the crest of the hill, I found myself at eye-level with the soldier's knees. He was wearing leggings. I was so close I could see the eyelets the laces went through. I got my feet under me and moved up silently behind him.

The dogs either heard me or smelled me as I

reached the soldier. The snarling halted and all of them started to bark. The soldier began to turn around.

I was right behind him, Hugo in my hand. I had planned to reach around his neck and slice his throat. I got my arm around his neck all right, but he fell to his knees, twisted over on his back, and started clawing on his service revolver. Neither of us spoke, but he was grunting with effort as he released the leather flap over the butt of his gun.

Swarming all over him, I grabbed the hand going for the gun. I brought the stiletto aiming for his throat. He twisted, panic in his eyes. Hugo's blade buried itself in his shoulder. I jerked it out again. The Chinese let out a short cry of pain and twisted. His hand jerked out of my grasp and now he had the flap of his holster open.

I reversed Hugo in my hand: raised my arm and quickly brought the stiletto down. This time I got the throat.

His eyes bulged and his hands dropped to his side. One of the dogs suddenly let out a mournful howl, its nose pointed to the sky. The others followed suit. The body under me quivered once, then was still.

There had been too much blood. I had taken too long. It was a sloppy kill.

I stood and wiped Hugo on the soldier's pants. I didn't want to strip the body, but I knew I would need some kind of uniform to get through that trap door. Finally I settled for the man's leggings and his parka. When I was finished, I retrieved the bear skin and covered him with it. Then I took my pack, my binoculars and the Winchester and slid down to the restless dogs.

The lead dog, a huge Husky, snapped at my leg and tried to go for my throat. I cuffed him alongside the head.

"*Hyaa!* Get back there!" I snarled at him.

He took three staggering steps back then, with another growl, attacked again, trying for my calf. We were fighting for authority that Husky and I. Sled dogs are mostly half-wild; they've been known to gang up and kill a man.

I kicked the dog and sent him sprawling into the sled. I cuffed three others who were snapping at my hands.

"Get back in line there!" I ordered. "Move! *Hyaa!*"

The big Husky sat beside the sled, snarling at me and showing his teeth. The others, I knew, would follow his lead because he was the strongest.

I stepped up and grabbed him by the back of his neck. He snapped and snarled and tried to turn his head to bite me.

"Settle down!" I ordered. I shoved him toward the front of the pack. He went sliding and tried to come back at me. One of the other dogs tried to snap at his back paw tendons. The big Husky turned on him and bit the dog's shoulder hard enough to draw blood. The other dog whined and backed away.

"Get back in line there!"

Reluctantly, the big Husky moved to the front of the pack. He kept turning his head, showing his teeth and snarling. But he knew. I was in charge. He hated it, but he knew.

When he was in place, I stepped up to him and

stuck out my mittened hand. His powerful jaws clamped down on it with a snarl. I kept the hand there pushing it further and further into his mouth. The strength of his grip sent pain clean to my shoulder. I waited until I felt his jaw muscles relax. His teeth parted, but I kept my hand in his mouth. He turned his massive head away and the snarls softened to growls. Finally, he released my hand completely. The growls quieted to whimpers.

I grinned and patted his thick, soft neck. "Good boy," I said quietly. "Good boy."

Then I went back to the sled. I picked up the whip. "Hyaa!" I shouted. "Get around there! Hyaa! Hyaa!"

The dogs moved off. They wanted to head straight, but I guided them around in a circle, heading back for the trapdoor. They barked and snarled and raised all kinds of hell, but they moved.

I reached forward to cover my back pack with a bear skin on the seat of the sled. As I did, I saw something under the skin: a small black box the size of a cigarette pack. There was a toggle switch on it and an amber light. Nothing else. I held it up in one hand while I cracked the whip over the dogs' heads with the other.

I was approaching the area where the trapdoor had opened. I had no idea how to get the damned thing to open, but I figured the little box might have something to do with it. Some kind of electronic device, perhaps, which either gave a signal to someone on the other side of the door or actually opened the thing itself. Anyway, it was all I had. From now on I would be playing everything by ear.

I held the little box in front of me and clicked the toggle switch. The amber light started flashing, and almost immediately I heard the crunch of ice breaking, followed by creaking and scraping as the huge trapdoor opened.

The dogs did not hesitate, but plunged right ahead for the yawning cavity. I dropped the whip on the sled seat and pulled the hood of the soldier's parka as far over my face as I could. The next minute, I had the same feeling in my stomach you get when on a roller coaster when you reach the top of a climb and start down.

The sled runners scraped on the ramp as we dropped down. Someone, I saw, was waiting for us at the bottom.

I turned my head slightly away. A Chinese Communist soldier stood beside a huge lever. As I watched, he pulled the lever down. The trapdoor screeched as it closed behind me. As soon as the door shut, the amber light on my little box stopped flashing. As I passed the soldier, he smiled and waved at me. We were approaching a lazy righthand curve and then we were in an ice cavern, its walls reinforced with steel beams. The curve straightened out, and the dogs pulled ahead. It was still too dark to really make out too much but ahead, along an arched corridor, I saw light, then other sleds and dogs. Mine started barking and raising hell as we approached.

My lead Husky knew what to do. He headed right for the other dogs and sleds. As we approached, he slowed down and eased my sled in between two others. All the dogs barked loud greetings. I climbed down and spotted a tray filled with raw meat to my right. I pulled enough chunks for the dogs and tossed it to them, making sure the biggest piece went to the lead Husky.

Eating quieted them down. I grabbed my pack and shoved my arms through the straps. Then I picked up the Winchester and moved off toward a narrow corridor to the right.

I heard again the sounds of activity going on in the caverns. The noises were hard to pinpoint; there was pounding and the *chunk-chunk* of machinery. Whatever the Chicoms were up to, it must have taken them quite awhile to set it up. They wouldn't welcome an intruder. There was one thing in my favor though. The lights along the corridors I entered were not very bright.

The whole area seemed to be a network of tunnels and caverns. I passed three caverns which held huge green machines which might or might not have been generators. Then I heard an unusual sound from close by: the gentle lapping of water. I headed for it.

As far as I could tell there was only one thing about me that set me apart from anyone else in the caverns—my pack. The men I passed were heavily armed, and they always seemed to be in a hurry. Most of them were soldiers of the People's Republic. They hardly seemed to notice me. Even so, I kept my face hidden as much as possible by the parka hood.

The gentle lapping sound was getting louder. I kept moving from corridor to corridor heading for it. The dim lights overhead were spaced about ten feet apart, and I almost missed the cavern entrance.

It was the largest I had seen so far, as big as a warehouse, and it was bustling with soldiers. As I stepped inside I kept the Winchester ready and hugged the wall just by the door.

It was brighter in there, but fortunately most of the lights were aimed away from me—at a wooden dock extending out to where water from the Arctic Sea lapped against it. Two Chinese submarines were moored at the dock, and two files of men were off-loading supplies from them. Huge crates were piled all around the cavern.

I moved away from the wall, edged up to the crates and ducked down behind them. I wanted to see how the subs had gotten inside the cavern. It was simple. Underwater lights lined the way to the mouth of a huge underwater cave drilled out of the frozen land. The subs came in underwater. When they were ready to leave, they submerged and went out the same way.

I tried to place the location of the valley from where I stood. If I was right then all these caverns and corridors had been cut out of the mountains shielding the valley. This particular cavern must be on the far side of the mountains, right on the edge of the Arctic Sea. But why? What was the purpose of this elaborate set-up? All these caves and armed soldiers and submarines? What were the Chicoms up to?

A loud-speaker blared and my head snapped up. The announcement came, loud and clear, in Chinese:

"Attention! Attention! There are two invaders among us! They must be found and destroyed!"

TWELVE

Sonja. The announcement had said *two* invaders, and the other one could only be Sonja. There would be no reason for any of the Eskimos in the settlement to come here, and Aku was too badly injured. No, it had to be Sonja.

She must have followed me. Maybe she found the dead Chicom soldier, and somehow discovered another entrance to the caverns. Then again, maybe she *didn't* follow me. Maybe she had spotted the man on the hill yesterday too. Whatever, the Chicoms would be on their guard now. I couldn't hope to go on being ignored for long.

The soldiers around me had stopped working and stood at attention while the announcement was made. Then they looked at each other, and about twenty of them marched out along one of the corridors. The others went back to work.

I figured I'd better get the hell out of there. I moved cautiously out from behind the crates and edged toward the entrance. I was moving with my back against the wall. I eased myself backwards around the corner to the corridor, turned, and found myself standing face to face with a young Chinese soldier. We were so close we almost bumped into each other.

His mouth dropped open. He started to bring up his rifle and drew in his breath to shout for help. But I already had Hugo ready. I stabbed the long blade through the soldier's throat. The shout died unborn. I jerked the blade out, pushed the dead soldier aside and moved quickly away.

I rounded a corner, sticking close, trying to avoid any more encounters. I didn't want to go back the way I had come; I wanted to find out what the hell the Chicoms were up to. The subs were used to bring in supplies. Except for cargo-hauling, they had little to do with what was going on there. Those supplies were being used for something.

I zipped through one cave after another, passing other caverns not quite as large as the dock-loading area. Whenever soldiers passed, I stayed in the shadowy area between the overhead lights. The corridors were not a maze; there seemed to be some kind of pattern to them. I decided they all must lead toward a central room or cavern. So, instead of jumping from one corridor to another I would follow one all the way to the end. It was possible that the answer I was looking for was there. I kept moving, close to the walls, the Winchester ready.

The corridor I was in did end in a cavern. From what I could see, it was larger than the dock area. I had started to enter when I heard a shout to my right. A shot was fired. The slug chipped away pieces of rock just above my left shoulder. I spun, the Winchester at my waist. The soldier who had fired was slamming the bolt of his rifle forward pushing another cartridge into the chamber. I fired first; the Winchester slug got him right between the eyes. The force of it snapped his head back and his body followed. His back was arched when he hit the floor.

I stepped quickly into the cavern and was just beginning to look around when I heard movement. I spun around and surprised another soldier entering the huge chamber. He started to raise his rifle, but I had the Winchester to my shoulder and cocked. My shot drilled into his forehead, flipped him backwards. He was dead before he hit the floor.

. I looked around again. The chamber was cold. Like the dock area, it was well lighted, but I couldn't see what it was . . . not until I looked up.

There were four missiles resting on launching pads close to the chamber ceiling. Looking past them, I saw the huge doors that would open to allow the missiles to be launched. These must be well-camouflaged from the outside. A launching pad for a fifth missile was under construction.

As I moved deeper into the cavern, I noticed the air temperature became warmer. I discovered five huge liquid storage tanks. I went to one of them and cracked the round valve handle just enough to get some of the liquid on my hands. I sniffed it and found it was some kind of fuel, possibly for the submarines.

I wandered further into the cavern. The thing was the size of a stadium. At the end of it was a huge atomic reactor. I checked the leads going in and out of it. The generators I had seen earlier seemed to be run by it. That meant this reactor was the only source of power in the caves. Besides running the generators, it must provide all the electricity for ventilation, lights and all the machinery. This was the cavern I had to blow. This was the heart of Ice Bomb Zero, the reason for my mission.

I peeled the back pack off and got to work. Taping up small packs of three sticks of dynamite each, I put one pack with a detonator and timer on each of the storage tanks. Next I put packs on each of the four launching pads. I set the timers for an hour—I figured in an hour I could easily be hell and gone from here. That was what I figured.

It had taken me about fifteen minutes to get the job done. I was surprised no more soldiers had entered the cavern. When all the explosives were planted, I went around and synchronized all the timers, resetting them and making sure they would all blow at the same time.

My back pack was empty now. I tossed it under one of the storage tanks and picked up my Winchester. Still no soldiers. I could see eight loudspeakers in the cavern, but not a word came out of them. I felt uneasy, as though something was about to happen.

With the Winchester in my hand I moved cautiously from the chamber to the corridor I had come in from. It looked deserted. What was even more weird was the silence. The machinery had stopped, the generators were not running—they must have storage batteries operating the lights and an emergency electrical system. I cocked my head, listening. Nothing. No sound. Only silence.

I stepped into the corridor and started walking. My boots slapped with each step. I felt I was being watched, but I didn't know from where. I passed the first overhead light and moved on. The second light was straight ahead. Then I thought I heard a noise. I stopped and looked behind me. Nothing. I shivered, as if a cold wind had blown down my spine.

And then I seemed to know. I was trapped and there was no way out.

I knew it before I saw the first soldier. He was about twenty feet ahead of me. He stepped out from one of the side corridors, his rifle was to his shoulder, aimed at me. Two more soldiers stepped out then. All of them had rifles aimed at me.

I spun around and faced three more. Two were almost hidden and had their rifles propped against the wall. The third stood ten feet away facing me. His rifle was to his shoulder.

I grinned and I knew it was a sickly smile, let the Winchester fall to the floor. Then I raised my hands.

"I give up," I said.

The soldier said nothing. He just pulled the trigger.

I jumped to the side, felt the slug rip into my right arm and push through and out. I felt a numbing pain, then a sharp stab that inflamed the whole arm. The slug had missed the bone but it chewed up a lot of muscle and skin tissue.

I spun around and dropped to one knee. I knew I would be dead in a minute if I tried to go for Wilhelmina. Instinctively I grabbed for the wounded arm. It was bleeding badly. I sat down and rested my back against the wall. My world became tinged with gray. I felt as if someone was sticking pins into me all over. My cheeks were cold, and sweat broke out on my forehead.

It was shock and I was fighting. Blackness, the blackness of unconsciousness, tried to take over but I fought it. Through the gray mist I saw the face of the man who had shot me. He stood above me, smiling coldly. One of the other soldiers asked whether they should go ahead and kill me. But the soldier who shot me didn't answer; he just kept looking at me.

"It is Nick Carter," he said finally. He knelt beside me and patted my sides. He found the armpit holster and pulled Wilhelmina out.

"Do we kill him here?" one of the soldiers asked.

"What do we do with him, Sergeant?" asked another.

The sergeant stood and looked down at me. "I think Colonel Chieng would like to see him. Get him to his feet."

They were not gentle. They grabbed my hands and forced me to stand. The prickly feeling had passed, and now I felt lightheaded. I doubted that I would be able to walk. I was on my feet leaning against the wall. Something warm was running down my arm, dripping off the ends of my fingers.

"March!" the sergeant ordered.

I started walking, my steps halting and stumbling. Two of the soldiers flanked me, each taking an arm. I howled with pain but that didn't stop them. I was losing blood, a lot of it, feeling weak, yet I kept thinking: they didn't find Hugo, or Pierre, my deadly gas bomb.

They marched me along one of the side corridors. There were doors here and there in the walls. Offices I guessed. We passed several before finally they

stopped marching me. We were standing in front of a
door with Chinese characters on it. Although I understand and speak the language to a certain extent, I
can't read it. The sergeant ordered five soldiers to
watch me, then opened the door and went in.

There were five rifles aimed at me. I felt I was
going to fall—my knees were rubbery. I pushed into
two rifle barrels and leaned against the wall.

The door opened again and I was shoved through.
I was in a small outer office with a desk, chair and
file cabinet. Nobody was sitting in the chair. The
sergeant opened another door leading to a larger
office. Two soldiers pushed me through.

The first thing I saw was Sonja tied hand and foot
in a chair. She strained against her bonds when she
saw me. Another chair was to the right of her. The
soldiers pushed me into it. I sat on the edge, my right
arm hanging limp, blood dripping from the fingers
making a small pool on the floor. I thought I should
do something about that blood. I reached over with
my left hand and found a pressure point. I pressed
and kept the pressure on. Taking two or three deep
breaths helped clear my head a little. The soldiers
filed out and the room was quiet. I raised my head
enough to look around.

Sonja sat watching me closely. I noticed a trickle of
blood at the corner of her mouth, and her parka had
been ripped down the front. Her left breast was bare
almost to the nipple.

I took another deep breath and looked around the
office. My head was beginning to clear now. In front
of me was a desk, and on the wall behind it a portrait

of Red China's leader. The floor was thickly carpeted.
There was one other chair besides those we sat on
and the one behind the desk.

Stationed on either side of the door leading in were
the sergeant and one other soldier. They held their
rifles along their right legs, muzzles pointing up. They
didn't look at us but at another door which I figured
must lead to a washroom, or maybe a bedroom. And
then the door opened.

The man who stepped into the room, wiping his
hands on a towel, wore the uniform of a colonel in the
Chinese People's Army. He had no eyebrows and no
head hair. He did have one large and well-waxed
handlebar moustache. His eyes looked like pencil lines
drawn under his shiny head. He was a small man both
in bone structure and height. I guessed Sonja was at
least two inches taller.

He dropped the towel on the desk chair and came
around to the front of the desk. For a moment he
stood looking down his nose at me. Then he nodded
at the sergeant and the soldier by the door. They left
their posts and took up positions on each side of my
chair. The colonel glanced at Sonja and smiled.

"Mister Carter," he said, his voice surprisingly rich
and deep, "We are honored that AXE would send its
top agent to find our little . . . shall we say, hide-
away?" He was speaking in English. "But I am a bit
confused. Perhaps you can straighten me out?"

I noticed that the knuckles of his right hand were
scraped. He kept rubbing them. I glanced over at the
blood trickling from Sonja's mouth, but I said nothing.

The colonel began pacing back and forth in front of the desk. "Mister Carter, let me explain my confusion to you." He stopped pacing. "Now here I have a lovely Soviet agent who has invaded our little operation here. And here, in you, I have the top American agent who has also invaded our ... shall we say ... home away from home. Is this coincidence? I think not. Are Russian and American agents working together?" He smiled. "I leave the answer for you, sir."

"We *were* working together," Sonja said suddenly. "But we aren't any longer. My assignment is to kill Nick Carter. I must see to it that he is dead before I return to Russia. He discovered that and we haven't been working together since."

Colonel Chieng stepped over to her. "That is very interesting, my dear." He stood, spread-legged, in front of her. Then, without warning, he swept his left hand around and backhanded her across the face. The blow echoed around the office. The force of it was enough to spin Sonja's head halfway around. Her chin dropped to her chest. Her hair screened her face from me.

The colonel turned back to me. "That was the same story she gave me before." He leaned against the desk in front of me. "You are strangely silent, Carter. Where is all this grand wit I have heard so much about?"

I said, "I found your toys, the ones you've been building in this little 'home away from home'. Four nuclear missiles, probably aimed for the United States, right?"

"Ah, so you *can* speak." The colonel chuckled. "The

missiles are programmed for *your* country, Mister Carter, and for the Soviet Union. Would you like to hear where they will go once they leave the launching pads?"

"Very much."

Colonel Chieng was as proud as a bantam rooster. I glanced at the two guards, then over at Sonja.

"There are flight patterns to Washington, to Los Angeles, to Houston, and to Moscow. We are constructing another launching site which will hold a missile destined for Leningrad."

"It's pretty dangerous telling us all this, isn't it?" I said, knowing better.

The area where his eyebrows should have been looked like two scars slanting upward. "Dangerous? I do not think so." He looked over at Sonja. "You may rest at ease about your assignment, my dear. I will see to it that it is carried out. But unfortunately, you will have to die with Mister Carter."

Sonja raised her head and shook the hair from her eyes. Her cheek where he'd struck her was bright red. "It won't do you any good, Chieng," she said. "Before I came here, I radioed my position to my superiors. They will be expecting me."

The colonel laughed. "That was a foolish statement, my sweet. We have very sensitive electronic sensing devices here, operated by an atomic reactor. It is possible for us to monitor every radio within fifty miles. You sent no message. You have no radio. The only ones who know you are here are the people in the Eskimo settlement—which we intend to wipe out just as we did that American base camp."

Sonja sighed and closed her eyes.

The colonel turned to me again. "And how about you, sir? Have you been watching too many movies like your companion? Are you going to give me some foolish reason why I cannot kill you?"

I shrugged. "All this talk is academic, Chieng. In forty minutes *all* of us are going to be dead. I found those missiles and I wired them with explosives."

Colonel Chieng chuckled again and stepped behind his desk. I could sense Sonja watching me. When I glanced at her, I saw something in her eyes I couldn't interpret. Chieng opened one of the large desk drawers. As I looked over at him I noticed Wilhelmina, my Winchester, and Sonja's Russian rifle on top of the desk. Then Chieng hauled out the little packages of dynamite taped together I'd planted in the missile chamber. I counted how many he laid on the desk. Four.

"You see, Mister Carter," he said. "We are not as stupid as you would believe. We knew you were in that chamber . . . we were waiting for you, remember? We did not think you were sight-seeing. My men found the explosives connected to the missiles. You have failed."

I smiled at him. "You *are* stupid, Chieng. I knew you'd find those explosives—you were supposed to. But that's only half of what I planted. The rest will be a little rough to find, and there's enough left to bring this whole goddamn mountain down around your scrawny neck." I checked my watch. "I'd say in about twenty-eight minutes."

There was silence in the room. I could almost hear Chieng's mind racing as he stood behind the desk staring at me. From the dynamite he had found, he knew what to expect. He knew what the detonators were like and the timers and the moment everything would blow.

He sat in his chair and reached under the desk. When he withdrew his hand there was a microphone in it. In Chinese he ordered a search of the whole chamber. His voice echoed through the corridors over all the loudspeakers. He repeated the order twice. When he hung up the mike, he looked first at me then at Sonja. But his face was blank.

I shrugged my left shoulder, and Hugo dropped into my hand. I kept my fingers over the stiletto, keeping it hidden. The soldiers flanking me shifted uncomfortably. I knew what they were thinking: If the whole mountain was going to explode, they wanted to be somewhere else.

Colonel Chieng stepped out from behind his desk. He stood to the side of it, his hand touched one of the drawer pulls. Then he sat on the corner of the desk and lit a cigarette. He seemed to be trying to make up his mind about something.

I was more concerned about how I was going to take out the two guards. I knew it would have to be quick—damned quick.

The colonel reached back and opened a drawer. He smiled at me. "Mister Carter, I am sure you could put up with a great deal of pain without complaint. I am going to try a small experiment. I wonder how much hatred there *really* is between you and this lovely Soviet agent." He nodded at Sonja. "I wonder how much pain you can stand to see her take."

He rose from the desk with something in his hand.

He was smiling. "I want to know where the rest of those explosives are planted," he said. Then, with his cigarette in one hand and the scalpel he had taken from the desk drawer in the other, he walked toward Sonja.

THIRTEEN

Colonel Chieng hunched over Sonja, blocking her from my view. She let out a low agonizing groan of pain. There was a sizzling sound as the colonel's lighted cigarette touched her. And then the scent of burnt flesh floated across to me.

No matter who she was or what she had planned for me, I could not let this happen. I swung my left arm in an arc in front of me. Hugo plunged deep into the chest of the sergeant on guard on my right. I grabbed his arm, pulled him across me and into the other guard. I was using my left hand; I didn't trust the right. As soon as the dead sergeant knocked into the other guard many things started happening.

Colonel Chieng straightened up and began to turn around. The second guard started to raise his rifle off the floor. I rocked forward across the small distance between me and the desk and got my left hand on Wilhelmina. Then I turned, and the room reverberated with the explosion of the stripped Luger. I had aimed at the surviving guard first. He had raised the rifle up when the slug ripped away his nose, and he pitched forward on the floor.

The colonel was reaching for his revolver. I shot

him twice, through the neck and in the chest. He stumbled backward, tripping over Sonja's chair.

The door burst open then and a soldier stuck his head inside the room. I fired at him, ripping away his right cheek. As he fell back I stumbled to the door, closed and locked it. I turned to Sonja.

The gray-blue eyes were smiling at me. "Are you going to kill me too?" she asked.

I leaned against the locked door. My arm had started bleeding again and the prickling feeling was back. I stumbled from the door over to the body of the guard I had stabbed. I wrapped my hand around Hugo's handle, pulled the stiletto out of the sergeant's chest.

Next I staggered over to Sonja. I went behind her chair and cut the ropes binding her hands and feet. There was a cigarette burn on her exposed breast.

I laid the still warm barrel of the Luger along her cheek. "If you get cute, I'll kill you," I said.

"Let's try to get out of here, Nick," she said simply. "We don't have much time."

"I don't trust you," I mumbled.

I picked up a piece of the rope and wrapped it around my right arm, used the handle of the stiletto to twist the rope tight.

"Let me help you, Nick," Sonja offered.

I shoved her away roughly. Stumbling away from her, I reached the desk. I picked up the Winchester and put my left arm through the sling, still holding Wilhelmina in my left hand. Suddenly I fell to my knees. I wasn't going to make it ... I had lost too much blood.

Sonja knelt beside me. "Please, Nick," she pleaded. "Let me help you."

I knew then I had to trust her, at least long enough for us to get the hell out of those caverns. I pushed myself to my feet, holding onto her. Then I nodded toward her rifle.

"Have to trust you," I said. I knew she couldn't kill me with an empty rifle. And if she could keep me on my feet, maybe I'd make it.

Sonja picked up the rifle. Someone was pounding and kicking at the door. I picked up one of the taped dynamite packages and peeled the tape off with my teeth. I had one stick in my hand when the door caved in.

I pointed Wilhelmina and fired twice. The office exploded with the shots. Then I knelt beside the colonel's body where his cigarette still lay smoldering. I touched the dynamite fuse to it, then heaved. I grabbed Sonja's hand and practically dragged her to the washroom. I barely got the door shut when it was ripped from its hinges.

The force of the blast was softened quite a bit by the time it reached us. I had been leaning against the door, and the pressure pushed it against me and back against the sink. Sonja went into the tub, sitting down hard.

I reached for her. "You all right?"

She nodded, picked up her rifle again and we went out the shattered doorway. What had been an office was now a shambles of fallen rock and ice.

There wasn't much left of the outer office either. All those who had been pounding on the door were dead, their bodies sprawled on the floor. We got out into the corridor and I checked my watch. We only had thirteen minutes left.

"How did you get in here?" I asked Sonja. We were moving down the corridor in a direction I hadn't been before.

"Were you lying about those explosives?" she asked, "Did you really plant them?"

I nodded as we trotted along. "Storage tanks. Fuel for the submarines." I was getting lightheaded again.

A soldier appeared out of one of the side corridors. He jumped in front of us and started to raise his rifle. I fired Wilhelmina, putting a bullet into his temple. The shot echoed throughout all the corridors. In a way that was good—it would make it rough for them to pinpoint our exact location.

"This way," Sonja said. She turned to the left into one of the branching corridors.

I ran a few steps, then stumbled. I staggered over to the wall and leaned against it. Sonja turned back to me.

Two soldiers appeared behind us. One of them fired, and the bullet hit the wall just over my head. I raised the Luger, which had suddenly become very heavy, and fired three times. Two shots killed the soldiers. The third was not a shot, only a click. Wilhelmina was out of ammo. I checked my parka for the spare clip. The Chicoms had taken it from me.

"Come on," Sonja said. She got on my left side and helped me away from the wall. "It isn't far now."

A weight was lifted from my left shoulder. Vaguely I realized that Sonja had taken the Winchester from me.

I stumbled ahead. Sonja had slung the Winchester over her shoulder; her own rifle was in her hand.

We came to a staircase. Sonja took my hand and led me up the steps. Each one seemed higher than the last. I kept thinking that the blast should have gone off in the launch cavern by now. Had they found the dynamite I'd planted on those storage tanks?

When we reached the top of the stairs, Sonja pushed a button in the wall next to a large steel door. The thing began to slide open. Immediately a blast of cold air hit us. It was like taking a bucket of ice water in the face. We were inside a short cave which led outside. As soon as we'd passed through, the steel door closed automatically behind us. We made our way along the rocky floor to the cave entrance.

The cave would have been almost impossible to spot either from the air or the ground. We emerged into late afternoon light between two rocks set very close together. We were about ten feet above the valley, and the ground was snow-covered and slippery.

I was getting weaker. For the first time since leaving Chieng's office, I relieved the pressure on the tourniquet. The loss of blood made every step I took an effort, and Sonja was down in the valley before me.

As I slid the last few feet to the valley floor, I heard what sounded like thunder. The ground beneath me began to quiver, then shake violently. I looked up and back the way we had come. The thunder rolled deeper and louder.

"Run!" Sonja shouted.

I staggered to my knees and pitched forward. I

scrambled to my feet again and ran after Sonja. The rumbling grew louder, filling the valley with sound. And then, suddenly the top of the mountain blew off. One of the shorter peaks seemed to lift like a crown. Flames blasted out with a roar. The steel door we had just come through buckled, shot straight out and skidded down the mountain toward us. For a second there was silence, and then the rumbling set in again but not quite as loud this time. Smoke poured out where the blast had torn away mountain walls.

Ice Bomb Zero was dead.

I watched the holocaust for a while, standing near the valley creek. Then I turned to look at Sonja.

She was standing about ten feet away from me, and she had her rifle to her shoulder, aimed at my chest.

FOURTEEN

I stood, weaving back and forth, almost too weak from loss of blood to stay on my feet. She was so far away and there was so little light. I could just see the shadows of her eyes, and her cheek pressed against the rifle stock.

"It is time," she said softly.

I figured I had one chance. I knew her rifle wouldn't fire. Maybe I could get to her before she found out it wouldn't. I took a step forward ... and sank to my knees. No use. I didn't have the strength. On hands and knees I looked up at her.

A light wind came whispering through the valley. Deep in the mountain, the rumbling explosions continued.

"I *have* to do this," Sonja said, but her voice sounded shaky. "It was part of my assignment. It was what I was trained for." She licked her lips. "Nothing makes any difference now, Nick." And now her voice *was* trembling. "We had to find out what the Chinese were doing out here. We did. We—you—destroyed the missiles. But this ... *this* is part of *my* assignment."

I was resting, saving myself. There was ten feet

between us and I had to cover that ten feet as fast as I could. I was not going to stay there on my hands and knees and let her kill me.

But she seemed to read my mind. She dropped the rifle from her shoulder and shook her head.

"Nick, I know this rifle won't fire. Why do you think I relieved you of yours back there? You thought I was asleep in the settlement? I was watching you. I saw you talking to the head of the village. I saw you empty the cartridges for my rifle and Aku's. And I watched you leave the settlement."

She dropped her rifle into the snow, quickly slipped her arm out of the Winchester's sling and brought the rifle to her shoulder. She looked at me down the barrel, not bothering with the scope. "I still wasn't sure what you had done, Nick," she said. "Not until I tried to fire my rifle while I was in one of those caverns."

I looked at her. So much woman. So much passion. And if I had any chance at all, that was it.

I said, "Sonja, before you shoot there are some things I think you should get out of your head."

She frowned. "What things?"

"Corsica, for instance. Forget the Calvi Palace. Forget the blue mountains. Forget my room with the crazy bathtub. And don't ever drink another Harvey Wallbanger."

"Stop it!" she said sharply.

"While you're at it, forget the fireplace in my cabin at the compound, the nights you came to me. Then there was that night in the tent when we went over."

"I said stop it!" She jerked the rifle back into her

shoulder. "Do you think I am an emotional fool? I am a Soviet agent. A good one. I will not fail."

She shook her head, steadied the Winchester. "For six months I have been training for this moment. I cannot fail."

I was so weak ... so weak. I couldn't think ... something ... then I remembered I had one weapon left: Pierre, my tiny, deadly, gas bomb, strapped to my ankle inside my boot. My hands and feet were hidden deep in the soft snow. I brought my feet forward and raised myself so that I was sitting on my heels. I reached back, got my hand inside the boot and around Pierre. I didn't want to do this, but Sonja was giving me no choice. I thought what we had done and what we had meant to each other, had meant something to her after all. I was wrong.

I said, "All right. Shoot if you're going to." But if I was going to die, she was coming with me.

She held the rifle steady, her finger on the trigger.

Then I thought of one last thing. "Before you shoot there's something I want you to get rid of."

She looked startled. "What?"

I was slowly maneuvering Pierre forward through the snow. "A bunch of guys aboard an American submarine gave you a ring. I want you to take it off before you kill me. You don't deserve to wear it."

For a moment I didn't think I'd made any impression at all. Then I saw her glance down at the ring on her right hand, the hand getting ready to pull the trigger.

In that instant I knew she wasn't going to kill me.

The Winchester dropped to the snow. Sonja cov-

ered her face with her hands and fell to her knees. "I
can't!" she cried. "I can't!"

I left Pierre in the snow and crawled to her. I
gathered her close to me and let her cry against my
shoulder.

"They—they told me you were a ruthless killer,"
she sobbed. "A maniac. They—they lied! You saved
Aku's life . . . you saved mine. And you have always
treated me with . . . with . . . How *could* I defend
myself against such tenderness?"

"Why should you want to?" I whispered. I brushed
the thick hair from her forehead, gently kissed an
eyebrow.

I said, "You know when you had that rifle I
couldn't see your eyes. And I wanted to see them one
more time . . . the way they sparkle with those little
gold flecks."

She wrapped her arms around me. "Oh, Nick!" she
cried. "I can't go back to Russia now. What will I
do?"

I gathered her close to me. "I'll think of something," I said.

We were still holding each other when the Eskimos
found us.

FIFTEEN

Sonja and I started building our igloo the next day. Since the slug I'd taken in my arm hadn't hit bone, all the Eskimos did was bandage the wound tightly. Raw fish, rest, and soon I was feeling almost normal. The arm was stiff and painful, but I'd had worse. In two days we just about had the igloo completed. Lok and his family offered to help us, but this was something we wanted to do ourselves. The ceremony was the reversed of usual procedure. Instead of having everyone around for the laying of the cornerstone, we had everyone gather round to watch us cut and lay the last block of snow on our little igloo.

Lok was there, and Drok, and Aku with his arm around the young girl I had seen in the community igloo, and most of the Eskimos in the settlement. We were about a mile outside of it.

The crowd stood by smiling and nodding as Sonja and I placed the last block on the igloo. I had to use my left hand which made more work for Sonja. We carried the block and slapped it into place, then leaned against our little shelter, smiling. The Eskimos gave us grunts of approval.

Aku stepped up to me, leaning on the crude crutch

the Eskimos had made for him. Half his face was covered with bandage. "I am glad this is the way things are," he said.

"So am I," I said, with a grin and a wink.

He looked embarrassed suddenly. "I have not thanked you properly for saving my life. It was a foolish thing I did."

"I did a couple of foolish things myself, Aku. But it's over now. Mission successfully accomplished." I looked at Sonja. "Well, the important part anyway."

The young Eskimo girl came to stand beside Aku. She tugged at the sleeve of his parka. Aku smiled at her, then turned and hobbled away, the girl beside him. The others too began to depart.

Sonja watched Aku walk away. She looked a little wistful. "Nick," she said, "do you think I will like living in America?"

"You'll love it."

"But . . . what will it be like?"

I kissed the tip of her nose. "We can talk about it tonight while we're laughing."

She frowned at me. "Laughing?"

"I'll explain it to you tonight. We'll have some raw fish, get a couple of bearskin blankets, light a couple of candles, and . . . laugh."

And that night we were alone in the tiny igloo. Outside another storm was building. The wind howled and whistled against the tiny structure. Somewhere a Husky howled.

We lay between two bear blankets, naked, close. We had made love twice already. Two small candles gave out a soft flickering light. I was lying on my left elbow looking down at her.

"I feel so ugly," she said, "with that awful cigarette burn on my breast. How can you stand the sight of me?"

I bent down and kissed, very lightly, the dark dot on her lovely breast. My lips moved to her nipple then away. "I pretend it's a beauty mark," I said.

Her eyes studied my face. "Nick?" she said softly, tracing my right eyebrow with her finger.

"Mmmm?"

"Why do they call it laughing? I mean, I can't understand how the Eskimos can call it that. When that final moment comes for me, I don't laugh. I kind of scream, and then I whimper."

"I've noticed," I said. "But maybe they mean you laugh on the inside, when you're with someone you want to be with."

She blinked her lovely long lashes at me. "I think I know what you mean. Did you see that young girl Aku was with?"

"I did."

"She is one of Lok's daughters. I understand Lok arranged it."

"Could be. They have many customs we don't understand."

"Are you laughing at me?"

I kissed the tip of her nose. "No, laughing *with* you."

She looked up at the ceiling of the igloo. "It's all over now. The Chinese used those submarines to bring supplies so they could set up an underground missile site. But how did they build those caverns to begin with?"

"Same way probably. The subs surfaced with digging machinery and the men to operate it. They just started digging tunnels. Must have been quite a while ago."

"But why didn't anyone see them?"

"This settlement wasn't here. Eskimos are nomads, they move around a lot. Radar doesn't operate that low. Maybe some scout from that American base camp discovered something and reported it, which was why the base was wiped out."

"Do you think they would have launched those missiles?"

I shrugged. "Maybe. More likely they would have used them as blackmail against both the Soviet Union and the United States." I started nuzzling her throat.

"Nick?" she said sleepily.

"Mmmm?" I caressed her flat belly.

"How long did you say it will take for a message to get out?"

"Well, it will take three days by dogsled to get to the nearest radio. By the time they get through the red tape and send a copter back to pick us up, it will take another day, maybe two. I'd say four or five days." I moved down, kissed her breast.

She wiggled a little and put her hand on the back of my neck. "Nick, darling," she breathed. "Don't you think we should be ... sending a messenger pretty soon ... now?"

"There's time," I mumbled against her softness. I raised my head to look at her smiling face. With only a little prodding, she melted those naked curves against me.

"There's ... plenty ... of ... time. ..." I said.

Nick Carter: the world's biggest selling spy series

If you enjoy Nick Carter

Meet Phil Sherman—top agent of the CIA

in a brand-new international espionage series
packed with suspense, excitement and sex

by Don Smith

SECRET MISSION: PEKING

Assignment: sell a black-market computer behind the Iron
Curtain. Simple enough, but when the computer arrived at
its destination it had developed an unplanned kink. Somehow Sherman had to get the computer back in working order
. . . so that it could blow up China's atomic centre before
Peking blew up the world.

SECRET MISSION: PRAGUE

Assignment: Sherman was to use his contacts to find the Mr
Big of European gunrunning. Just point the way to the
mystery man behind five million dollars' worth of arms,
destined for every black ghetto in America. After that the
professionals would take over for the dirty work.
But espionage is not that simple. . . .

SECRET MISSION: ISTANBUL

Assignment: kidnap from the Red security prison, the
beautiful nymphomaniac wife of Soviet master spy, who is
only too willing to betray his country in return. Sherman
becomes the unsuspecting pawn in a game of double-dealing
and death between East and West.

SECRET MISSION: TIBET

Assignment: destroy the lethal laser beam operated by
Chinese scientist, that is destroying both American and
Russian manned space flights. Sherman finds more than the
death ray in the ancient Buddhist monastery. Among its
captives is an unrepentant ex-Nazi, a traitorous American
scientist, and a beautiful blonde.

Tandem editions 25p

Occult and the Unusual in Tandem editions

Name...

Address ....

Titles required ....

....

....

....

....

....

....

....

The publishers hope that you enjoyed this book and invite you to write for the full list of Tandem titles.

If you find any difficulty in obtaining these books from your usual retailer we shall be pleased to supply the titles of your choice – packing and postage 5p – upon receipt of your remittance.

WRITE NOW TO:
  Universal-Tandem Publishing Co. Ltd.,
  14 Gloucester Road,
  London SW7 4RD